PRAISE FOR THE

"Every once in a while a piece of fiction comes along that can change the way we think about the world. The Awareness is one of those transformational novels—it's a wonderfully written book that tells an entertaining and suspenseful story, but even more, it would be almost impossible to read this book and not come away with a new and heightened understanding of the human-animal relationship."

> Bruce Friedrich, Senior Director for Strategic Initiatives at Farm Sanctuary, Member of the advisory board of the Christian Vegetarian Association

"The Awareness is an amazing book—partly because it's such an extraordinarily gripping story, but also because I can think of no other recent novel that explores the minds of animals with such sympathy and compassion. I would recommend this book to everyone I know—and hope they recommend it to everyone they know as well."

> Nathan Runkle, Founder and Executive Director of Mercy for Animals

"Every now and again I sit back and wonder what it would be like if other animals could really fight back against the egregious violence to which we subject them in a wide variety of venues ranging from research laboratories and classrooms to zoos, circuses, rodeos, factory farms, and in their own homes in ours and in the wild. This thought experiment takes life in *The Awareness* and reflects their points of view, and it's clear they do not like what routinely and thoughtlessly happens to themselves, their families, and their friends. By changing the playing field Gene Stone and Jon Doyle force us to reflect how we wantonly and selfishly abuse other animals and the price we would pay if they could truly fight back. This challenging book also asks us to reflect on the well-supported fact that we need other animals as much as they need us. It should help us rewild our hearts, expand our compassion footprint, and stop the reprehensible treatment that we mindlessly dole out."

Marc Bekoff, Professor Emeritus of Ecology and
Evolutionary Biology at the University of Colorado,
is the co-founder, with Jane Goodall, of Ethologists
for the Ethical Treatment of Animals and the author
of *The Emotional Lives of Animals, Wild Justice: The
Moral Lives of Animals,* and *The Animal Manifesto*

"What a wild ride this book is! The writing is so beautiful and it was a doorway into animal consciousness. This novel stirs up every dark fear that what we do does indeed come back to us. Stone and Doyle may have just written the next iteration of Planet of the Apes..."

Kathy Freston, bestselling author of
The Veganist and *The Lean*

"*The Awareness* develops a powerful theme first orchestrated by Arthur Machen in his book *The Terror*, and tells of a time when animals become self-aware and rise up against the tyranny imposed on them by humans in virtually all areas of animal use. Although I have been a strong and relatively successful animal advocate for 40 years, and as such well aware of the injustices and thoughtless atrocities we impose upon our fellow creatures, this book touched me very deeply, and opened wounds in my soul I thought healed, or at least scarred over enough to protect me from acute pain.

"Told from the perspectives of numerous animals we humans interact with—a dog, a pig, a bear, an elephant and others—we are inexorably drawn into the hurt, resentment, anger and bewilderment which these innocents experience with the coming of 'awareness.' It is particularly the latter that hurts me as a conscientious reader, the fact that there is so rarely an answer to the question 'why?'; 'why am I being beaten, confined, starved, deprived of companionship and love, forced to do unnatural things, mutilated surgically, and the rest of the countless abuses I suffer silently?'

"And there is no answer.

"This a book all those who care—and all those who don't care—about animals must read."

Bernard E. Rollin, professor of philosophy, animal sciences, and biomedical sciences at Colorado State University and author of *Animal Rights and Human Morality*, *The Unheeded Cry: Animal Consciousness, Animal Pain and Scientific Change, Farm Animal Welfare*, and *Science and Ethics*.

The Awareness

Gene Stone and Jon Doyle

the
STONE PRESS

Library of Congress Catalogue in Publishing Data
Stone, Gene & Doyle, Jon
The Awareness / Stone, Gene & Doyle, Jon

ISBN-13: 9780615944647
ISBN-10: 0615944647
1. Domestic animals—Fiction. 2. Vegan Cooking. 3. Animal protection. Animal welfare. Animal rights.

Library of Congress Control Number: 2014930043

Printed in the United States of America

2 4 6 8 9 7 5 3 1

The Stone Press
New York, New York

Contents

A chimpanzee in a laboratory in an eastern city notices the silver latch. He jingles it. He reaches around and jingles the silver lock, too. It's loose. Then he tears the lock off and opens the stainless-steel cage. The men in white lab coats look up from their clipboards, surprised when they see the animal running toward them.

The impalas and the cheetahs lead their assault like an amber armada. Running swiftly, they tear into tourists on safari and locals selling goat meat at the market. The impalas ram into the humans with their graceful, streaked heads. The cheetahs finish off the wounded.

A herd of bison from somewhere on a high plain charges a small general store in the Dakotas.

Water buffalo gore Vietnamese day workers in the peaking heat of a low-country rice paddy.

Three lions with biblical manes, escapees from a zoo, stalk the streets of Rome.

A black-and-white orca swims in circles around a Plexiglass pool in the light-blue haze of a Southern California theme park. The bodies of two trainers float like broken dolls near the corner.

Five llamas attack a group of young students reading Borges in the high altitudes of Lima.

All over the world, mammals attack. They are remembering. They are thinking. They are planning. They are becoming aware. It doesn't come to each the same way, with quite the same echoes, with quite the same soft or hard edges. But it comes to all in one way or another.

The revolution is at hand.

I

BEAR

THE BEAR sat in the shallows of a river. He wanted salmon. He always wanted salmon. One of the fleshy silver fish jumped out of the water, as if on demand, and the bear caught it deftly. He devoured it. A little residual carnage remained on his paw, but he'd fed and it was time for him to sleep.

The bear—brown, thick, and healthy—lived in the northern Rockies, surrounded by white peaks and severe blue skies. The trees towered over the cold river and the snowy peaks towered over the trees.

A hawk circled overhead, screeching. The bear didn't notice. He didn't care much for hawks.

Somewhere, not too far away, a gunshot penetrated the frigid air.

The bear froze. The sound was familiar, but he couldn't remember why. He knew the name for it because the names for everything were flooding into his head, and he knew he didn't like it. Something about it was wrong. His mind clouded, and he shook his head, hard, as though to dispel the fog, the haze.

A hare raced out from the evergreen thicket. The bear could think of nothing else now.

The hare bounded over the rocks, the drifts, with skill and grace. The bear chased him without grace but with skill and tenacity. The two animals drew a maze in the snow, and crossed a river whose bubbling, cold waters ran fast. Each leapt over a fallen tree branch.

The bear won. He captured the hare.

Another shot, from somewhere in the woods, behind the bear.

The hare was trembling in the bear's paws. His eyes were open but the time for seeing was over. He waited.

Nothing. The bear held the small animal carefully. He smelled the salmon on his own claws, he smelled the hare's fear. He picked at the hare, he studied him. Soft belly. Big ears. Warm fur.

I had a mother, the bear thought.

He didn't remember ever having a thought before. He didn't remember remembering. He'd just been.

The hare blinked. He was about to be killed and suddenly, he seemed to understand. Death. Not just the end of running. But death.

The hare trembled in the bear's claw. The bear looked at his prey but didn't eat.

The bear was remembering his youth. He was raised in a den, not far from where he was now, that had a stale scent, slightly damp, mildewed. He had an older brother. His mother was magnificent–large, dark, warm. She gave him food when he couldn't find it himself. He remembered reaching up, trying to steal the salmon from her paws after she'd caught it and brought it to him and his brother, who'd waited at the river's edge, playing in the shallows.

She lowered the fish to him and let him tear into it as if he'd caught it. She let him think he was the mightiest hunter. That day, and all days at the beginning, she was patient with him, teaching him the rituals of the chase. He followed her every movement, crouching low to sneak up on the berry patch or the beehive or wherever she wanted him to practice. He would try his best to emulate her, ears up, nose sniffing for the right scent. But his legs were not agile enough to crouch as she did. He'd fall over and roll down hills when he was supposed to be stalking. This amused more than angered her. When he came bounding back up the hill, ready to try again, she'd nuzzle him close and he loved the feel of her fur against his, like the feel of that first summer wind blowing in off the river or the den at night when he was tired and knew it was safe to sleep.

"She taught me everything I know," he said to the hare.

The hare's eyes were now closed.

A gust of wind came from the south and the hare's ears doubled over, one of them hiding an eye.

The bear studied the creature, shivering but not moving. He used his free paw to lift the hare's ears off that large, bulbous eye, which was darting frantically from side to side.

"I want to find my mother," he said. He wanted to find his mother. Again he remembered his mother's fur, the smell of the trout on the brittle ends of her paws, the way the sun shone bright and high upon both of them in the spring. He wanted to find that simple day that had long since passed. More than just finding his mother, he wanted to find himself with his mother. He wanted to be little again, rolling down hills, preparing to be what he was going to become.

The bear sat down. He knew that day could never be found, as sure as so many suns had set. The bear wasn't prepared to feel the weight of time. He could feel it passing, moment by moment, and he wanted to make it stop.

The hare had calmed down, his body shifted slightly. He watched the odd behavior of the bear with keen interest. "And I want to live," he said boldly.

The bear found his legs again and stood up. He let the hare go.

The hare paused at the bear's feet, unsure of himself. Then he bolted away.

A cold drizzle began to fall, east to west, not west to east. This had never happened up in this part of the world.

The hare, before reaching the woods, turned and looked at the bear.

"Thank you."

The bear nodded.

Then the hare was gone.

The brown bear, six feet tall, four feet broad, sat down on a log near the river. He put his paw to his mouth. He licked it. It tasted good.

I want to find my mother, he thought again and again. The thought became more than a thought. It became an obsession, and it made him feel warm in a corporeal part of him he couldn't define.

So he set out to traverse his complex land. Starting from the creek, he walked west, toward the orange-and-grey sun balancing just above the horizon. He grabbed a salmon because it jumped up and fell in his paw. He ripped its head off and ate it without thinking.

Further west, he came to a river. This river wasn't babbling. It was roaring. The bear roared too, his whole body expanding. Not even the water could contain him. He crossed the river, fighting the current easily.

In the middle of the river, he dunked his head in the frigid liquid. Under water, he closed his eyes and let the coldness wash over him.

I also want to find my brother, he thought.

He waded out of the river, drenched but determined. As he shook off the water saturating his fur, he heard a loud noise. It stung so much he put his large paws up to his ears.

Humans.

He knew of them. He'd seen them. But only much further downstream.

He lifted his nose. They were close.

His instinct was to leave, not to care, but he remembered the gunshots he had heard earlier. Then another image flooded his memory, roaring in like the river when the ice melted, and it hurt. The image was from some time in the recent past. Not long ago he'd come across an aged elk, walking without precision, the fur under his large neck grey and matted. The elk wasn't behaving like an elk, she was moving in jerks and pushes. She was dying.

The bear followed the elk. Soon, the elk tired and collapsed in a clearing. The bear walked up to the elk and heard her breathing rise and fall as her nose pressed against the dirt. It didn't take long for a blanket of swollen flies to surround the wounds and the elk's eyes went calmly still, and she died. The next morning, the bear passed by the clearing. The elk was no longer there. The forest had taken her away.

The bear sat by the edge of the river. He wanted to leave again. He thought about his mother. He wanted to ask her questions. She'd taught him everything he thought he'd ever needed as a bear, but she never taught him how to understand. He wanted to understand the carcass of the elk. He was afraid of the image, of the calm, dead eyes and the movement of the flies as they descended upon the creature like wildfire on the pines that then fall, dried and brown, to the ground.

Upriver, two humans were snowmobiling. The sight was odd but the bear remembered seeing something like this before.

The humans wore bright red jackets, ski caps, and goggles, and shouted at each other.

Above, the hawk was still circling. The hawk screamed and the scream echoed, so much so that the bear stared up at the sky, watching the bird watching him.

The roar of the snowmobile drowned out the hawk's cries. The machine was throwing snow on all sides. The bear's eyes narrowed. He felt his chest quiver but he wasn't cold.

The engine noise neared. The bear crouched lower. But he didn't attack, he let the humans glide past on their machines. After they were far away, he waded into the water. A shiny liquid lay on the snow. It reminded him of the lights that lit the sky in the heart of summer. Slick and filmy. He dipped his paw into the oily substance and tasted it. He knew he shouldn't do this. But in the spirit of curiosity, of the strange newness that had enveloped him, he took a chance with a foreign substance.

Horrible. It lacked the sweetness of honey and the weight of salmon. It was too warm and burned his throat.

Ahead was a large sequoia. He walked to it uncertainly, his gait ungainly and awkward. Then he vomited. He looked at his mess, cocking his head. This had never happened before. He took note that there were limits to his new powers. Once the poison was out of him, he stood up on his hind legs and raised his long arms into the air. He took in the air, a deep breath, and he felt good.

He decided he was going to find his den. Not his current den—that was back east of the river. His old den, the one that always had the scent of dampness and where he lived with his mother and older brother. He walked a long way, but he didn't tire. He walked and walked. Finally, walking up a steep hill, sensing familiar objects, he felt he must be close.

He heard something growl in the thicket.

He stopped. He'd made a mistake. He'd crossed into the territory of another bear. He had never done that before either.

The other animal, glossy and black, tore out of the thicket. Bigger and stronger, he rose on his haunches. His roar echoed against the valley's walls.

The bear's first instinct was to fight back, but his second was to run.

He couldn't recall having had a second thought.

The black bear charged, and the bear raised up, ready to take that charge. His claws were poised. These new thoughts meant nothing in the face of another bear's claws. The black bear bore into him, pushing him down, knocking the wind out of him. The bear lay on his back, and the black bear slashed at his body. Oddly, he didn't draw blood.

"I'm sorry," the bear said.

The larger bear stopped. "Why?"

"I don't know."

"Why are you here?"

"This is where I grew up."

The black bear rested on his haunches. Neither animal smelled hostility. They breathed easily.

The black bear sniffed. "There's something odd on you, something I haven't smelled before."

"It's salmon. Of course you've smelled it before."

"It smells different."

"I may have had some trout, too."

"Something else."

"I touched the snow after the humans ran their machines over it. It looked interesting. I tasted it."

"You should not do that. You are young."

"All I want to do is find my den. My mother."

The black bear pondered this.

"And then what?"

"Then maybe I will understand."

"Understand what?"

The bear didn't have an answer to that question.

"Then I will leave and not come back," was all he could think to say.

The two bears looked hard at each other, adjusting to the sounds of their voices, their own words. Then the bigger and stronger one nodded. He let the bear enter his territory.

"Go and find her. Then leave." He lumbered off, his black coat thick and glossy.

"Thank you," the bear said.

The bear remembered the path that was only a few feet from where he was standing. It led to where he'd grown up. Where had this knowledge come from? Had it always been there, resting in his mind? What other maps existed in his head?

He walked from the river to the path that led to the pinnacle of the mountain, the cave. Much had changed. The meadow where he and his older brother had tousled and sparred and fought to be the better cub was overgrown with weeds and saplings. As he walked further, the path still flat, he remembered the three trees beyond which his mother had made it clear that he and his brother could not cross unless she was with them.

The trees had aged. They were still magnificent, but they had grown older. He had never thought about age, but he remembered his brother daring him to step over the line, and he did, but his mother's roar sent him scampering back to his brother, who laughed. His brother was a year older than he was, and larger, and he was always trying to get him into trouble.

The path started to steepen. The smells had changed. Or was that just because it was summer now, not spring? The scent of wildflowers and thawing ice and beginnings was gone, replaced by staleness. Nothing sweet to savor.

He lumbered up the path. His mother had told him to keep his den as high as he could, and he had lived by those rules ever since. But he'd forgotten how high this was. He was breathing heavily, panting and walking more and more slowly. He saw a large boulder and climbed it, to take a rest, to look at the country above and below.

Perched upon the large slab of granite, he looked past the crest of trees and into the blue sky. Vapors of clouds formed a tufted arrow towards the north. He noticed the hawk still circling just above the tree line. Hawks should circle higher, he thought. How can the hawk see his prey; more importantly, how can the prey not see the hawk? Strange bird, the bear thought. The hawk let out a screech, then another. The sound hurt the bear's ears, and he suddenly felt that the cry might mean something. Was it a warning? He shook that thought off. Hawks and bears have no interaction.

He looked down at the land below, where he could see the other bear hiding behind a wilting evergreen. The other bear was too large for the tree. The bear climbed down the boulder and began traversing the steep mountain yet again.

All of this climbing had made him hungry, and now he regretted letting that hare go. He decided to forage. He checked for traces of the other bear with his eyes and nose, but found nothing. There was a wild berry patch not too far off where he and his brother used to sneak away to devour the tart fruit. He went into the woods, turned right at the tree his mother had marked. He sniffed for her scent—it wasn't there.

He was nearing the spot where the berries had been when he smelled something wrong, something lying behind the base of a tree. Curiosity got the better of his hunger. He veered left, away from the berry patch.

A dead bear. Headless. The carcass atrophied, much of it eaten away by rodents and birds. What once was robust and alive was now frail and torn apart. First he remembered the elk, now he had found a bear.

The bear sat down and stroked the stiff carcass. He sniffed. For one quick moment he thought this bear was his mother, but no, the bear was a male. His brother? He felt himself losing his breath at the thought of it.

He turned the dead, headless bear over and inspected what was left of his body. His brother had several black rings just above his paws. How many times had his brother tried to gnaw those rings off, never understanding that they couldn't be licked or bitten away? No rings on this bear.

Then he looked closely at the bear's chest and saw three black holes. This was different from the elk, who had had no holes, only grey fur and a worn antler spike. The holes were ugly, crusted over. He looked up to see if the hawk was still trailing him, but the hawk had vanished.

Back on the trail, climbing up and up, he spotted the cave. He sprinted for the opening, now covered with dirt and small rocks, the result of some sort of mudslide. When he reached the cave, he stopped, rising up on his hind legs. He sniffed something, something he hadn't sniffed before, but he let the strange scent go and tore through the wreckage, his huge paws swiping.

Swipe after swipe, he removed large quantities of the sediment blocking his path. A part of him was aware that his mother and brother wouldn't be in there. It was summer and the three of them had all lived in the cave so long ago, but he needed certainty. Anyway, even if his family wasn't there, he wanted to sit in the place they'd all once been.

When he left the cave for the final time, he had never thought he'd be back. His brother had left before him and never returned. The bear knew he'd do the same. He proudly left the cave, left his mother, rumbling down the hill. When he reached the line that his mother had forbidden him to cross, he turned back briefly, out of respect for her authority, and saw his mother watching him go. Her eyes indicated that he needed to move forward. He did.

It took longer than he expected to clear the opening of the cave. The rocks grew bigger and bigger as he dug, his swipes slower.

Finally, using his snout, he nudged his way into the cave.

Silence. He sat down and looked around. It was so much smaller. Or he was bigger. The odors were unfamiliar, with a hint of decay. The damp smell that he wanted to smell again was replaced by other animals' scents, maybe a fox's or a wolverine's. But he was glad to be home. He rested his head against the curved wall and, before he could remember anything else, he was asleep.

He awoke hours later, stomach growling. He felt as though he could have been asleep for a few moments or a day. He stretched his arms and legs. The berry patch was just a short hike from the den. The odors and tastes filled his mind—the sugary smell of the bushes in the summer heat, the syrupy flow of the berries trickling down his throat. He licked his lips with his flat tongue.

He trudged out of the cave, trampling over the shrapnel from his digging. A sharp shard of rock pierced his paw as he attempted to brush it away. The bear was patient but had no tolerance for such petty gripes as a cut paw. He put it to his mouth and licked at the blood. He could still smell the salmon and suddenly the berries didn't seem appetizing at all. His stomach was sending an unassailable message to his brain. Eat.

He started down the path and came face-to-face with the black bear, a gash over his left eye, patches of his pelt conspicuously missing. He's an old warrior, the bear thought, and here I am, bemoaning a minor cut.

"Did you find her?" the black bear asked.

"No. I found nothing."

"I could have told you that."

"Did you know her?"

"Maybe. Who knows? Who knows anything?"

"I am beginning to know many things."

"If you know so many things, why were you stupid enough to come into my territory uninvited?"

"My thoughts told me to."

"What good are thoughts if they put you in danger?"

The bear thought again, and then thought about thinking, and it hurt his head.

"I don't know." He felt the way he did when a salmon wiggled its way out of his grip and fled upstream.

"You're young. You'll learn."

"Learn what?"

"To not think so much."

"But I've never really had these kinds of thoughts before."

The black bear stopped and pondered this. He'd never stopped to ponder before either, but he didn't want the young one to get the better of him.

"It doesn't matter. You'll just learn."

"I hope so." The two beasts stared at each other. "I'm starving."

"The river's free territory. Go to the big black spruce upwind. The salmon were jumping like fools there. I've had my fill. But no foraging. This is my land to forage."

The bear lowered his head in acquiescence.

"Thank you for letting me see this place."

"I don't know why I did it. Now leave, as you promised."

"I'm leaving. I won't eat the wild berries."

The black bear whipped his head around. "What berries?"

"Over past the fallen log and the dead bear."

"How did you know of that place? That's my secret spot."

"I told you. This is where I grew..."

Both bears froze. Overhead, the sky was suddenly dark with fowl. Hawks, ducks, geese, wrens, jays, a blanket of birds pulled west, toward the city. An odd wind blew leaves off the trees. Field mice scurried back and forth, unseen but ceaseless, the forest floor shifting noisily.

"What's going on?" the black bear asked.

"I don't know, but I smell something I've never, I..." He couldn't find the word.

"I know. What is it? It's not food. It's not a female. It's something. It reminds me of the dream I had. I know, but I don't know," the black bear said.

Three moose charged through the dense forest. Then a family of deer. Hares.

"Should we follow?" the bear asked.

"Bears don't follow," the black bear said.

Then the younger bear said quietly, "I know what the smell is."

"Tell me."

The bear couldn't just tell him. The word that came to his mind was complicated. It was about the dead elk dying so differently than the dead bear. It was about the humans, but it was also about the den, and his brother and mother. It was the feeling that he'd lost them forever, his home and his family. And even more, it was about the fear that not only had he lost them, but that they might have been taken from him, stolen.

"It's the smell of war."

The bear went off to feed his ravenous stomach, leaving the black bear to wonder why that word smelled so bad.

Elephant

I got a feeling called the blues, oh lord...

The truth was, she knew it was going to happen. She knew before anyone else. She knew because she believed she'd willed it to happen, in her darkest hours, as the trailer lumbered down a back road, her body aching from the journey that never seemed to end. She had lived through so many beginnings and so many middles, and she knew that, at some point, she needed an ending. So when the awareness came to her, she was ready for it.

Since my baby said goodbye...

The yellow light of morning leaked through the slats of the cage that clung to the rig rumbling down the lonely highway. Her big, sad eyes, black with brown flecks around the iris, peered through the emptiness between those silver slats. The land was flat, so flat it almost seemed to be eternal in its yellowness, and then her black eyes with the brown flecks peered up as best as they could and saw the sky. Blue going up forever the same way the yellow went flat forever. She tried to find where the yellowness and the blueness met, but she couldn't–the metal trailer blocked the connection. She blinked.

The elephant heard voices from inside the truck. The radio was playing.

All I do is sit and cry...

Nancy the elephant (her first trainer had given her the name) knew the scene in the cab all too well. She had listened to these conversations many times before, but today she listened more intently. Today she understood.

Nancy knew the men who were conversing. The one who wasn't driving liked to spit into the large red cup; the other one disapproved.

"Disgusting habit," the driver said. Nancy liked him well enough. He had been driving her for years and years. He was big for a human, barn-like; his greying mustache hung below the edges of his lips. But Nancy was wary of this man, and of all the men and women who drove the trucks and fed her and locked her up.

"Come on, Hillbilly Hal."

"Quit calling me that," the driver said.

"Hillbilly Hal. Hillbilly Hal."

"Quit it."

"Okay."

A pause. Then, "Hillbilly Hal."

She had heard this back-and-forth bantering for years and had wondered what it was about. Now, she was disappointed. It was about nothing.

The younger passenger laughed. Nancy heard a shooting sound and knew that the younger passenger had spit the black liquid into that red cup yet again. "I'm hungry. When do we get there?" the spitter asked. His odd, high-pitched voice irritated her, hitting her ears like a whine.

"You sound like my granddaughter, Jake. It's just a few more miles."

Unlike Jake, Nancy didn't want to get to where they were going. Still, she hated being where she was now, and so she listened to the talk, and to the song that played amid the banter, the back-and-forth sounds that helped kill a little bit of her current burden, even as they pressed her forward toward a burdensome future.

Jake didn't take the bait. "Hillbilly Hal," he said. "Who the hell is this old man and that goddamn twang? Damn."

"It's Hank Williams and it's my favorite. Anyway, what else we gonna listen to?"

"I don't know. Anything. Talk. The news."

"What the hell do you care about the goddamn world?"

"Something," Jake muttered.

Nancy heard that familiar sound of spit.

Nancy tired of the men's conversation. She looked along the side of her trailer and saw a gale of dust blow across what had been flat, yellow land. Behind that was another truck, then a semi, then two more vans, then more semis. Nancy knew the formation, the steel caravan moving through the scorching heat of the northern Texas desert. Nancy knew that Hal and Jake, leaders of the caravan, drove straight and slow, the older man quiet now, listening to his song, the younger one looking out the windows the way kids on the verge of manhood do— with equal parts wonder and disgust.

Nancy turned away from the maelstrom behind her and maneuvered her body around the small cage. Her size was majestic, her trunk snakelike, her head a mosaic of tiny grey tiles, a mural of alien beauty. Her ears, which listened intently to her drivers, were sad, like her eyes, and sponge-like. They hung loose, but she could stiffen them in an instant. That was her gift. She could be both loose and solid.

She'd been on the I-27 before, but this was the first time she had felt more than just the hard road; she saw more than the dust clouds. Each bump and divot was a portent of something waiting just down the road. Yes, she knew before anyone: she knew the minute the road ended, the rest would begin. In the back of the truck, amid the stench of hay and feces, she was planning. She was more wary of her surroundings than ever, and she was watching and recording.

"Where are we?" an animal, all nasal squeak, asked.

"On our way to the next destination," Nancy said. She tried to hide the weariness in her voice. She was tired of destinations that led to nowhere. She felt the awareness was going to be different, she was sure of it, but she also knew that she didn't know enough to make any promises, to herself or to the goat.

"What?"

"I said, we are approaching our next destination. And we're almost there. The truck is slowing. Or it will soon. I can tell. The other trucks will slow down. And then the work will begin."

"The work? I would love to do work." His voice softened.

"You're a little goat. Why would you love to do work?"

"Because then they'd all come to see me the way they come to see you. No one cares about me. No one likes a goat."

"I like you. I always have. I see something in you."

"What?"

"You have a relentless nature."

"I have nothing." Something occurred to the goat. "We've never done this before."

"Talk?"

"Is that what it is?"

"Can you understand the song?"

The goat thought about her question. Then, very slowly, the goat shook his head. "I know you mean the sounds coming out of the cab, but I can't quite understand."

Nancy guessed that awareness must be different for each mammal, that it might have something to do with how much direct interaction a mammal had with humans. But that was only a guess. She decided to help the goat along.

"Tell me about yourself," Nancy asked.

Before the goat could answer her question, the trailer stopped.

"Now we get fed, before they put us to work," the goat said. "Well, you get put to work. I get to eat dried hay in a small pen and wait for children with dirty little hands who just point and stare and laugh."

And then it was as if an odd light had turned on inside his head. The goat stopped and looked up and out through the slats, the way Nancy had earlier. The awareness was growing stronger. Nancy watched the goat realize it. He sat down and looked first to his right and then to his left.

"They are all so afraid of us," the goat said of the humans, in wonder. "They fear us now. But not our people, these people here. The war is waging, but they don't know, do they?"

"So you see it now?"

"I do," the goat said. "I see. I also see that you see more. Why?"

"I don't know. Maybe in the same way some humans are kinder to us than others. I think it's different for every mammal," she said and then paused. She had a friend once; his name was Edgar. They slept, chained to the wall, in adjoining stalls. He was a stubborn bull of an elephant.

"Yes," Nancy said again.

He paused. "But how come the humans don't know yet?"

"How could they? While we've been back here on the road, in this trailer, the heat too much to bear, stepping in our own feces, they've been ignoring the world, they've been–"

"Let's attack the minute they open the door. You crush them with your foot. I'll attack them with my horns." The goat was giddy with excitement.

The elephant shook her head.

"We must act normally."

"Why? We should fight like the others, like every other animal."

"No," she said, with force.

"They're coming," the goat said, and Nancy focused on what was happening outside of the trailer.

The men in the semis, men just like Hal and Jake, teeth stained with coffee and cigarettes and eyes red with methamphetamine, jumped down from their cabs and walked to the rear of their rigs and rolled up the large steel doors with weary hands. Nancy was familiar with the clanking of metal on metal.

She heard the other animals murmuring in their cages, restless, their awareness growing, their readiness apparent.

One of the weary men, the one who had alligator-like skin and veins running down his neck like a junkie's dream, called to Hal, who was sitting on the back of the trailer marked *Elephant*. Nancy could smell the depression on Hal. She suddenly felt sorry for him.

"Hillbilly, how's the kid?" the man asked. Nancy recognized him by scent more than by sight; she knew he'd been around even longer than Hal. That menthol odor belonged to him alone.

Hal gave the old-timer the middle finger, a human insult Nancy had seen many times.

"I would hate to have to coddle the owner's son," said the older man.

"When do the trainers get here, Sam?" Hal asked.

"Hell if I know," said Sam. His menthol scent bothered Nancy. "Do you know when those assholes get here, Bill?" The man named Bill, who'd joined Hal and Sam, shrugged his narrow shoulders.

"What the hell. How are we supposed to start setting up without them?" Sam asked.

Jake, the owner's kid, sidled up, straw hanging out of his mouth. He rolled it over and over with his tongue. "You drivers crack me up. We can do whatever we want."

"Get that Huck Finn bullcrap out of your mouth," Bill said.

Overhead, a blackbird circled. Nancy couldn't see it, but she could sense the bird, watching.

Menthol Sam squinted up at the sky. "What the hell is that fella doing here?"

"Who the hell cares about a bird, Sam?" said Jake. "Let's get this built."

"Against the rules," said Hal. "Need trainers present."

"Forget the rules. Just forget 'em," said the kid.

"The boy's right," said Sam softly. "We should just get it over with. Get the tent up, get the animals fed, set up the cages. Then we can go into town."

"Not on my watch," said Hal.

"Damn you, Hal, my dad's your boss." Jake pounded the trailer. Inside, the goat ran under Nancy's belly. She let the goat seek comfort under her. For a moment her dreams welled up inside, but she pushed them back. She kept her big eyes on those slats, on the blue sky and the yellow land, on the men, their blue eyes and yellow skin.

Hal went to the kid and slapped him hard. The kid fell back and then lunged forward. The two other men, Menthol Sam and Bill, watched. Nancy felt a surge of tension, as Jake, also relentless and ugly, rose and circled the older man. He still had a bit of chew left and spit it in the dust near a rock. A black-necked garter was sleeping there, but the spit didn't bother the snake or his sunbath.

Both men had their arms up. Nancy had seen fights before, fights that broke out amid the haze of lives lost on the highway, lives lost on fourteen-hour drives from town to anonymous town, every Wednesday or Sunday or Friday. The men were detached from everything but each other; they were a brotherhood built from knowing nothing but put 'em ups and take 'em downs, and tired animals performing exhausted tricks.

Jake struck first. His punch was quick and weak, nervous, the one he had to just get out of the way. The punch landed on Hal's shoulder. Hal countered with a left jab, then a right hook, and the fight was over.

"We wait for the trainers. Like regulation states."

"What was that?" the goat asked.

"Nothing."

"Did you notice how the other two just stood back and watched?" The goat pranced when he grew excited. The noise of his hooves bothered Nancy's sensitive ears. With her long trunk, she calmed him down.

"Humans like to watch, don't they?" the goat said.

"No. Those humans are predators," Nancy whispered to the goat.

"How? They have no kill in them. All they have is their weapons and whips. Get them naked. They have nothing."

How could she tell the goat just how dangerous they could be? She needed him to believe that the mammals had a chance at victory, but she needed to warn him too. It was a delicate game.

"They have eyes that point straight ahead. Those are the eyes of a hunter. But not a great hunter. You're right."

The goat was silent.

"Prey have eyes on the side of the head," Nancy added.

"We need to kill them then. The revolution is happening. We need to join."

"Goats don't kill."

"Now we do."

Nancy wondered if she had been given so much thoughtfulness, so much memory, so much sorrow for a reason. In the wrong hands this new awareness was dangerous. The goat was too eager. He was thoughtless. He would bolt out without thinking, he would jerk and jolt, leave himself vulnerable, and die.

"Plus," Nancy said, as if the goat had heard her last thought, "we're trapped in this trailer until the trainers come anyway."

The goat grew impatient. "We have to join in."

Nancy shook her head. "We need to get the tiger and the lion out first. We need to match predator with predator. If I attack, I can get two or three before they aim a gun at me. But they can't fight the lion and the tiger."

"How do we let them know that?"

"The lion and the tiger understand what's happening. They understand combat."

Nancy shifted her attention to the men outside. Through the holes in her trailer she could see the old man, Menthol Sam, sitting on the back bumper of the trailer.

"I remember when the circus was billed as a sort of paradise," he was saying. "When I was a kid, it's where we went when we had nowhere else to go. It was our church."

"What century was this, Sam?" Hal asked, laughing.

"It was this magical place and people revered us," Sam said.

"I don't believe you," said Jake. "My dad talks like that too, but you old guys are doing what old people always do. Forgetting about what it was really like."

"What a sad worm you are, Jake. People did revere us. We had a place to be revered and for most of us that was something special. The crowds came to our shows by the hundreds. They wore their best clothes and sat in awe as the lion tamer came out and whipped the lion around the cage and the horses pranced and the trapeze artists flew over them. Without nets."

"I remember that, Sam. I remember it well," Hal said. "It was nice back then. Now everyone's on a drug." The two older men shared a look of nostalgic silence.

"Who cares about all that?" the kid interjected, smoking drag after drag off his cigarette.

Nancy cared. She remembered setting up those circuses. The poles too heavy for her to lift, but she did it anyway. She had no choice. She remembered the beatings, and the lions' abrasions and the horses who disappeared when they could no longer prance at just the right tempo. She remembered everything the old men romanticized.

She was beginning to care less and less about what the humans were saying. She had been listening to humans for too long. Knowing the meaning of their words only made the sounds of their voices more intrusive, more frustrating.

The blue hadn't faded from the sky, but the yellow land was turning beige, almost brown. The blackbird was still circling, but higher now, so that it looked like the foil to a star, a black twinkle.

Nancy turned away from the men for the final time. She wouldn't listen again.

"I'm afraid of them," the goat said.

"Why?"

"I wish I had your size. When we attack I will be the first to go."

"No. I'll look out for you."

A pause.

"Are we friends, Nancy?"

"Yes."

"I don't remember," the goat said.

"What don't you remember?"

"How I got here. If I'm going to die, I wish I could remember everything, and all I remember are bits and pieces. My mother's milk. My first show. But everything else is shady and full of fog."

"Maybe I can remember for you. I recall when you arrived. We were in Dallas. The goat before you died and you could do what she did."

"What did she do?"

"Bark on command."

"Dogs bark."

"It's an expression."

"I wish there was another expression for goats."

Nancy didn't know what to say. She knew that the men would be feeding them soon, whether the trainers arrived or not. Food was regulated now. When it wasn't, how thin had she become, that first summer, when she first met Edgar...The blight of a heat wave, the humid New Jersey air, and the hunger. It overtook her, like the heat. It consumed her. She begged for food as best she could, dropping her head low and submissive, but they wouldn't give it to her. Not until she'd learned to bend down on her hind quarters.

"Nancy? Why do you have a name and I don't?"

"You already answered that. People come to see me and they come to pet you. A big beast who can stand on one leg and spray water and bend down needs more than what a petting animal needs. She needs a name."

The goat bleated. "I'd like a name."

"I'll give you a name then." Nancy studied him. "Your name is Joe."

The goat bleated. "Joe!" He liked it.

"Nancy?"

"Yes, Joe?"

"If all the animals are taking over, why are we even going to another show?"

Nancy pondered this. Her ears perked up. She tilted her head. "Because we haven't taken over yet. It's just beginning."

"How did this even happen, Nancy?"

Nancy smiled.

Then, Nancy and Joe sat in silence because the men outside had become silent. Nancy gazed out through the metal slats. She saw the men putting out cigarettes and dispersing like cockroaches under a neon light. She wanted to know exactly what the lion and the tiger were thinking, and the horses and the baboons, and the giraffes and the smaller monkeys, and then she said to Joe, in a soft but firm voice: "The trainers are coming. And they know. I can sense it. It's almost time to fight. Are you ready?"

"I am," said Joe. And he was. He was knocking his head back and forth like a fighter before the bell.

"We will have to ambush them, all at once. The others know."

"How do you know that?"

"I just do, Joe."

Joe quit shaking his head. Nancy could sense his fear. She shared it. They both knew what the predators outside their metal cages were capable of; and now they also knew that neither talon, nor claw, nor tooth, nor poison was stronger than an active mind.

The trainers were approaching. The trainers always came sometime after feeding. Nancy looked outside of her trailer, through the slats of metal, and she could see the horizon that she'd been trying to find earlier. There it was. A simple line connecting the sky and the land, connecting two things that she didn't think had anything in common. She lingered on the image. Then, she turned to Joe.

"Are you ready?"

He couldn't speak. He nodded, a very human gesture.

"Friend. It's time."

Dog

A nighttime gust, heavy with the grime of an upstate New York heat wave, whipped freshly cut shards of grass into the air. The blades were swept up, a swarm of green gnats attacking the fading moonlight, then retreating, turning, turning, and falling silently to the ground. An old-fashioned push mower, its dull blades painted red, bent over itself like an old man in the middle of the yard. Next to it was an open shed housing other grounds-keeping tools: a rake, large clipping shears, a broken-down leaf blower that rested tiredly against the oxidized wall, a half-empty plastic gas tank, and toolboxes of varying sizes, along with an old notebook where plans for a new landscape design had lain for years, nothing now but remnants of faded ink.

Near the shed, a small craftsmen-style home with second-story windows jutting from the roof was framed along the bottom with wooden boxes full of crimson geraniums and pink impatiens. A large porch wrapped around the first floor. A hammock idled empty in the languid wind. A bike lay against the cedar-wood siding. More potted plants—succulents and ferns—dotted the porch.

Behind one of the second-story windows a woman, Jessie, was sleeping soundly, half under a sheet and half exposed, her arms twisted around her body as though seeking protection, making her look younger than her thirty years, her long brown hair tangled in the pillow, her sockless feet dangling off the bed.

And then, it started—a strange sound, coming from the shed. A squeak. A few more squeaks. Then a flurry of taps up the sides of the shed. The tapping stopped briefly. And then a thud on a windowpane, just above the geraniums. Two more thuds.

Tapping again. Bodies squeezed through a cracked window, bodies that shouldn't have fit, penny slots giving way to silver dollars. Three more soft thuds on the carpet of the upstairs bathroom. Then the sound of scurrying, of small victories, of rodent steps.

The three rats stopped at the doorway. They conferred about what to do next. The leader, the one with the longest tail, nodded his head and the other two understood. They contorted their bodies so they could pass underneath the small space between the door and the hallway's wood flooring and then slinked their way down the corridor.

They approached the first open door where the leader peeked inside the doorway. He heard the rhythmic breathing, felt the inertia in the body, and knew the human was sleeping. Then he saw the foot, exposed, ripe for attack, primed for the bite and the revenge of those sharp front teeth.

"On three."

The rat counted down.

"Three," he said.

Two.

One.

And they were off. Ready to attack. Their eyes weren't the dead black eyes of sewer rats. These eyes possessed passion, ferocity, and purpose.

His eyes were shut, but he was awake. He could feel the hardness of the floor instead of the usual comfort and calm of his worn fleece bed back home at their old apartment in Manhattan. He missed the corner that Jessie had designated for him, the corner where the sunlight was softened by the half-open blinds and the taller building next door. When the warmth hit him as he slept now, it was just a tickle of heat. He missed his corner.

The hardness of the floor was worse than ever because Jessie had taken him to the groomer a few days prior, where the horrible woman with the breath of spoiled meat had shorn him down to nothing for the summer, his brown-grey hair piling up on the floor.

"What is he?" the woman had asked. "He looks part shepherd, part hound, part everything else." Jessie just shrugged while he stood in the tub, water running down his shaved body. His long ears drooped low as the woman prattled on and on about the death of fleas and the comfort brought on by dog shears. Grooming made Cooper less hot, but it also made him just less. He felt naked and exposed then, and he felt naked and exposed now.

He turned over, trying to find relief. But something else was making him uncomfortable. He was aware. But the awareness wasn't hitting him with full force. It danced with him, alerting him to his lack of fur, and to the weight of his breath, entering his body, circling his lungs, and exiting once again. He knew what wind was, he could discern the hardness not just of the floor, but of the air too, of everything; he noticed angles—acute, obtuse, perfect angles—and the variations in Jessie's breathing patterns as she slept; he could sense the outside, but he had no desire to go there. He had no desire to go anywhere. He shut his eyes.

He had never dreamed like this. He was walking proud and tall on two legs, not as some parlor trick to make an owner feel like a master, learned through the trial and error of doggie-treat tribulations, but as a functioning biped. He did this for what felt like a long time, walking to and fro. With his head higher, he felt a surge of pride. He looked through a window at the city scene that lived beyond the glass. Another dog was walking down Avenue A. Also as a biped. She had a bouquet of flowers in her paws. He wanted to go and walk with her. She was promising him something, and though he didn't know what it was, he knew he wanted it. He gained trust in his legs, and then he rose up off the ground, floating four feet in the air, and turned slowly on an invisible axis, without gravity, without falling. The window disappeared, as did the dog with her flowers.

Then his primal senses overcame his sleep. His eyes opened, his nose twitched. His ears perked. Cooper could smell the intruders. The scent didn't alarm him as it might have in the past, though it was rank like the groomer's breath.

Then, in a flash, he saw the rodents' motion, their teeth bared, aimed at the draped foot, Jessie's foot.

Not a second's hesitation: he leapt toward them. He could feel his teeth, the flare of incisors. His breath was heavy, air tickling his lungs, then spewing forth. His nose was wet and twitching. A part of him seemed to be watching himself from above instead of the rats down below.

The leader of the rats jumped back, avoiding Cooper's paws and teeth. The other two halted, and the three rats rose up on their hind legs, making themselves seem bigger than slipper size.

"What are you doing?" the leader asked, frustration filling his voice.

"I could ask you the same."

Cooper remained in the attack position. He wasn't relenting, although a part of him wanted to. A part of him could smell the foot, the human foot, the stink of it. He had always smelled this smell on humans, he realized. But the way he interpreted the scent seemed irrevocably altered.

"That's it," said the third rat. How did she know what he was thinking?

"Smell what we do. Go on. Take a bite." The rat grinned, exposing a row of finely sharpened yellow incisors.

"No," said Cooper. But he wanted to.

"If you won't, we will. Stand back."

"No." Cooper puffed out what fur he had left, momentarily hating the groomer and then, forgetting her, bared his teeth. Hot, angry drool dripped to the floor.

The rats hesitated, but instead of retreating, they scattered in different directions. Cooper dropped his head and tried to follow all three at once. He lost sight of each. The leader jumped on the small bedside table, where the blinking red lights of the alarm clock flashed on Jessie's face. The second rat darted under the bed, the quickest access to the other side. The third rat ran in a circle, stopping in front of Cooper, acting as the diversion, the martyr.

Cooper paused just long enough for the third rat to open her mouth wide and sink her teeth into the bony flesh of his right front leg. Cooper yelped in pain and panic; then, the initial shock passing, he lunged with his own teeth, found the nape of the rat's neck, grabbed her, and shook her body back and forth.

He'd done this before. To toys. Rubber things. And now he was doing it to this rat, this breathing object that lay powerless in his bite. She tasted like felt-covered peanut butter. He could feel the rat dying as she squeaked in pain. And then the blood came, trickles of it, coating his tongue and rolling down his throat. Repulsed, Cooper dropped the rat, silent and still and dead.

The leader watched from the bedside table.

"You kill one of us and more spring up from the shadows," the leader said.

The second rat appeared on the other side of the bed. "Now we feast."

Both rats scurried toward Jessie, still asleep, her headphones keeping her impervious to the battle.

The leader had reached Jessie's neck, but Cooper used his tail to flick the rat off a split second before his teeth would have made their puncture.

As he did this, the other rat dug under the heavy cotton blanket, looking for the exposed skin of Jessie's stomach. Cooper pounced on the blanket; he could feel the rat trapped between the blanket and the mattress. But the rat was quick, relentless. He squirmed until he reached the bottom of the mattress, dropped to the floor, and regrouped.

The leader, having been flung off the bed by Cooper's tail, was back on the bed and sprinting towards the woman's neck once again. Cooper leapt, smothering the rodent with his body, and was, for the second time, bitten hard.

The rat jumped off the bed and joined his compatriot.

"Why are you stopping us?"

Both rats were panting.

"Because you're attacking her."

"As should you. As should we all."

"This human is my life. I would die for her."

He had a fleeting image of himself, in a cage, his puppy teeth gnawing at the price tag attached to his small, opened cage, his fur imbued with fleas, devouring him like a virus. And then Jessie, grabbing him, pulling him close to her, hugging him, not afraid of the fleas. Not even aware of them.

"You don't have to understand. We do. We've understood this since the dawn of time. They are to be hated, bitten, turned to ash."

Morning sun streaked through the window like a harsh yawn.

The rats glanced at each other, made a mute agreement.

"We'll be back," the leader said. "You better understand by then."

Cooper stood guard over the sleeping body as he watched the rats leave. The corpse of their friend lay in the corner. Neither rat acknowledged it as they vacated the room.

Cooper remained still for at least a full minute. He could sense the rats heading outside, back down to their home in the shed. Finally, when it was safe, when he knew they were out of the house, he sniffed around Jessie, checking her body, smelling it, rubbing his nose against it, making sure she hadn't been hurt. Once satisfied, he jumped off of the bed. He licked her outstretched foot and nuzzled against it, proud to have been its savior.

Then he approached the dead rat, picking it up gently with his teeth and carrying it downstairs, through Coop's Door, as Jessie called it, to the backyard. There he found some loose soil where Jessie's mother, Carol, had been doing some planting, and dug a small hole. He dropped the rat into the hole, covering him up with the dirt.

Cooper hung his head as he looked at the mound.

"He's dead. I killed him."

Cooper had chased rats before back in the city. How many times had he kept rodents away from the apartment? How many times had he frightened them from trash bins, from holes in the wall, those small grey pests with the beady eyes and unremitting determination to encroach on Jessie's territory? First on Avenue A where Jessie lived in a tiny studio, and then when she moved to a nicer neighborhood uptown after she'd finally landed a good job. But mostly, he chased them when she moved in with Peter, who had a duplex apartment on West 15th street—until two weeks ago, when Peter left Jessie, and Jessie left New York City, and now the two of them, Jessie and Cooper, were living temporarily at Carol's.

"He deserved it," Cooper said of the dead rat, convincing himself. "I was protecting Jessie. That's my job. That's what I've always done."

But he felt hollow, his skin pliable and full of holes, rattled by the wind.

"What you've always done is no longer important."

Cooper didn't realize he was talking aloud until he heard the voice respond. He turned.

"Clio."

"Cooper."

The tortoiseshell cat walked close to him, rubbing her tail against his fur, pressing her body softly against his chest. She sniffed the mound that housed the dead animal.

"We need to go now," she said softly.

"Go where?"

"To join the others. But first we need to think of a reason for this," she said, pawing at the mound, scratching up some dirt. "The others won't take kindly to the fact that you've killed one of our own."

"How can you call a rat one of our own?"

"How can I not?" The cat and dog looked at each other, eye to eye. Cooper knew just how many rodents Clio had killed.

"Don't talk to me about what I've done in the past," she said. "The past is dead. What we do now, everything we do, is about our future."

The sun was ascending in the eastern sky. The insects had begun their morning chorus, but there was no rejoinder from the morning jays and mockingbirds. From inside the house,

Cooper and Clio could hear Carol clamoring about. Pots and pans and brewing coffee.

"Cooper, we can't stay here."

The phone rang in the kitchen. Cooper raised his ear and heard Carol answer.

"I think we both know that's not a gossip call to talk about who needs a new hip," Clio said.

"What do you mean?"

"It's happening. Humans are waking up and they are talking, emailing, texting. The revolution has begun. Do you think Jessie is going to fight for us? Do you think she's going to betray her people?"

"How can you talk like that? Jessie saved you from the streets as much as she saved me."

"That was in the past."

"The past matters."

"Not now. We no longer belong to them. We belong to ourselves. And the future."

Cooper's mind heard and understood Clio's words, but he fought them off. She saw this. She knew the first battle she would have to fight was right in front of her.

"Quit trying to find reasons to love her," Clio said.

But Cooper couldn't quit doing that. It was more than just collars, belly rubs, walks in the park. It was the way she grabbed his nose, pretending to gnaw it, laughing. It was how she spoke to him in a private language that no one else understood, not even Peter. It was the way she made room for him on the bed on the coldest nights in January and how he could feel her next to him, her breathing steady and thus steadying his own breathing.

"You can't stay. I can't stay. Not any more. It's not safe. We need to join the others, to mobilize, to fight."

"I have to think. I have to think. I have to think." He panted the words.

"Cooper. The last thing the world needs is a dog who overthinks."

Cooper kept silent, causing the impatient cat to rub against his body once more. She pushed him a little, putting him off balance.

"Why do you rub your body against everything? I've always wondered."

"Why do you open your mouth and drool all over the house?"

"Why do you make that strange purring noise?"

"Why do you wag your tail all the time?"

He changed gears. "I cannot go without saying goodbye."

"Okay. Goodbye. Then we go."

Cooper instinctively sniffed her nose and then, backing off, used words. "Agreed."

Clio led the way, Cooper close behind. They reentered the house through the pet door, both trying to act as normal as two animals with this new awareness could. Carol was still on the phone, whispering inaudibly into the receiver, still in her floral nightgown and plush slippers. But her body was tense, her back rigid. Her whispers sounded like hushed shrieks.

"She knows," Clio said to Cooper. "She knows."

They stole past Carol and climbed the stairs, silently, Cooper looking at the photographs that lined the hallway, celluloid nostalgia, Jessie at various stages of development: a toddler in floaties splashing in a kiddie pool; an eight-year-old birthday girl sliding down a slide, arms raised, carefree; a teenager at her first formal dance, awkward smile silver with braces, hunched shoulders towering over the nameless boy who stood grinning with his floral boutonniere. Her graduation from high school photo, her graduation from college photo. The photos of her and Peter. There weren't any photos of him and Peter—Cooper was always Jessie's.

"Cooper," Clio said with force. "Make it quick. Say your goodbyes. I'll meet you downstairs near the door."

"You're not saying goodbye?"

"Cats' actions are our words."

She wasn't sure why she said that because the fact was, she wanted to say goodbye just as much as he did. But she couldn't admit it. Something inside was talking to her about ancient deserts and hunts and things that she had never thought about before, but seemed now to be as much a part of her as Jessie.

Both animals paused on the steps, unsure where this journey was leading. Cooper moved first. He turned and slowly walked up the rest of the stairs, then down the corridor to Jessie's room. Each step felt heavy on his paws.

He stood for a moment before entering. This was where Jessie had grown up, and it still was a girl's rather than a woman's room. Carol had kept it as it was, this animal-themed room, filled with stuffed beasts, all with those dark eyes that, though inanimate, seemed to blink as if they were going to come to life at any moment. Cooper had never paid any attention to them before, but now it was all he could do not to rouse them from their sleep, to see if they would come and fight and join the fray.

Jessie was up. She was waiting. Her eyes were burning. "Cooper," she said. "Is it all true? I read about it online. It must be. Is it?"

He didn't know what to say. He had waited his life for this moment. So many times in the past he had felt so close to being able to speak to her. He often felt he was speaking to her through his groans and barks and whines, through his tail and his eyes and his legs. Yes, he didn't have awareness like this before, but he had felt something so close, moments when the awareness he did possess was only limited by his inability to communicate it. And he suspected Clio had felt something similar; and perhaps all the other animals had felt they were just a step or two away. Just that close.

Now that he could talk, he didn't. He jumped up on the bed and nuzzled her. He licked her hand, cherishing the salty smoothness.

"Say something," she said.

He wanted to say that he knew when she was going to move or flinch or yawn before she knew.

"I'll start. From the beginning. Do you know I loved you from the first moment I saw you in that horrible cage? I'd wanted a poodle. I was desperate to get a poodle. Then I saw you and I haven't thought about a poodle since."

"I love you, Jessie," he said.

She started to cry. "I love you too, Cooper. You've been with me longer than anyone. You're the only constant in my life. I don't think I ever quite realized that until now. But you've always been there. Always."

Cooper looked into her eyes. He could feel that breath again, entering his body, then exiting. He could feel the essence of being alive. He could feel something he'd never felt before: the consequence of action. Leaving meant more than just going someplace else. It meant leaving something behind.

She knew.

"Don't go, Cooper."

Cooper felt his heart; he actually felt it hurting. "I have to," he said. He had thought talking to Jessie would be the most wonderful thing that could happen. It wasn't.

"No," she said.

I have to stay, he thought. But he also thought, I have to go. He could sense Clio waiting by the back door along with his destiny. If he acted now, he could still meet it. If he waited just one more moment, if he spent one more second with Jessie, he would never leave.

"I'm sorry, Jessie," he said.

Without looking behind, he left Jessie pining on her bed and went downstairs.

But Clio wasn't where he thought she'd be. Cooper sniffed the air, trying to locate her scent. He couldn't. Had she left without him? Perhaps she had gotten a bit of a head start; that was something Clio might do, even before the awareness had set in.

He put his snout to the thin, plastic door, but it didn't push out. Something was blocking it. A wood plank, which kept Cooper from going out and anything else from coming in. The skunk plank, Jessie had called it.

He felt a twinge of fear. Had Clio done this? Locked him in somehow?

He went to the back door. There he found Carol, locking it. The two made eye contact.

"Where do you think you're going?" Carol asked.

Cooper couldn't stop his low growl. Carol had never liked him. Whenever Jessie came to visit with Cooper and Clio, Carol tolerated the pets, but only out of love for her only daughter. Everything else, from the food she gave to the truncated love she proffered, indicated a woman who wished there were no animals.

Carol moved around Cooper and walked diagonally toward the kitchen. She rummaged through a few drawers, using her hands as her eyes, her actual sight never wavering from the shaved dog near the sliding glass door.

Upstairs, Cooper could hear Jessie stirring.

He wanted to leave the house before she came down. He couldn't face her again; he couldn't say goodbye for a second time.

"I have to get out of here," Cooper said.

"I bet you do. You think I don't know what your kind has been up to? The deaths? Not here. Not in my home," Carol said.

She had found the object of her search: a small, silver pistol, a gift of protection from a long-dead husband. With shaky hands dotted with liver spots and spider veins, Carol pointed the gun at Cooper.

Pig

Her hoof slipped on the sodden floor. It was damp from washing, clean now of feces and fallen slop. Her eyes were on her hoof, but it was what she heard, not what she saw, that preoccupied her. Noise everywhere: squeals, grunts, groans. They came from her neighbors, from the machines, anywhere, everywhere: high-pitched, loud, loathsome. She had always heard them but now she *heard* them. They sounded foreign and frightening, like giving birth, like taking life, and they hurt her ears. She did her best to ignore these sounds, as well as the other sounds: the hum of the temperature gauge; the clicking of the feeder troughs; the clanging of metal. The din of the world she knew.

Her hoof slipped again. She realized that the ground wasn't level here; it receded slightly, so that slop and feces ran into the metal-grated drains in a small parcel of floor at the center of the pen. She stared at the drain, the place where the discarded things fell, never to be seen or heard from again.

"Pig," she said as she caught herself.

The word felt good as it escaped from her mouth into the air. She let her tongue escape too, she let it wet the area just outside of her snout. She was beginning to feel warm. She was beginning to feel hot.

"Pig," she said again.

She was pressed against an iron fence. She let the metal of the fence dig into her pink flesh, branding her, and although it hurt, although she could feel her hoof slipping again, she kept herself pressed against the metal to fight off the vertigo that was overtaking her. She began to feel as though that drain, the sewer, the hole in the floor, were destined to take her, to swallow her into their mysteries, pulling her down with the waste and vomit and excess.

"Pig."

She kept herself locked against the fence for as long as she could, but inevitably the pain of the metal overtook her fear of the grated floor.

Amazingly, she didn't slip. She didn't get pulled down by some unseen force. She remained where she was. And she thought, for the first time, about who she was: a pig, one of scores of pigs, big breathing pink beasts, packed together, moving almost as one entity made up of many parts. All of them with wild eyes, staring at each other, screaming at each other in a new language—this was the noise she couldn't understand, she realized. A language teeming with semantics and syntax, void of the groans and grunts of her past.

She glanced over the slew of bodies surrounding her. Had she never seen the large, silver walls of the pen, towering fifteen feet high? Had she never noticed that the pen was actually cut in half by a dirt path, that each half was gated by the same metal that had bored into her skin? How many of those just like her were in here? This large room? How many? She lifted her head. Too many. Too many replicas, and for a second she thought perhaps it would be better to fall down the drain, to slip into the ether, which had to offer more solace than what she saw before her. The claustrophobia of the awareness, of her particular awareness, was powerful and scary.

She dropped her head and closed her eyes. She thought of the sun. Then she stopped herself. What was the sun? She felt close to remembering it, the sun, but no image entered her mind, no matter how hard she tried to conjure one. Maybe the sun was a myth, and not worth this effort.

And then she thought of one word: "Human." But the word wafted away like a secret....

"Focus," she told herself. "Focus on what's here. Hoof."

Her hoof. She lifted it. It was harder than the rest of her. It seemed to be made of ivory bone; she licked it. It held the taste of salt. In the middle, it was cracked, like the pen itself. She noticed the symmetry of things. The fact that it was split evenly pleased her. Above the hoof was her leg, short and strong and dotted with coarse hairs and stains from something she didn't recognize. Above the leg was her body. She could feel the weight of it; it was heavy. It seemed *too* heavy.

"Pig," she said.

"Why do you keep saying that?" asked a pig next to her.

"It feels good to say it," she responded, trying not to stare at the other pig's large, dark eyes.

"Pig. Pig. Pig," the new pig said, then fell silent. She seemed to be waiting for something.

"See?" the first pig asked.

The new pig shook her head.

"Maybe you're not saying it right." She looked the new pig up and down. She noticed something sticking out of her left ear. A tag. With a number on it. She inched her face closer.

"What are you doing?" the new pig asked.

"You're number 789."

"I am?"

"Yes. That's what it says. On your ear."

"Pig 789. I like how that sounds."

Pig 789 then looked at the ear of her new friend.

"323."

323? Yes, she thought, good. The digits belonged to her, like her hoof, like her stout legs. Amid the pen of replicas, she owned something unique.

"Pig," she said again. But this time the word came out like lava, slow and powerful and hot.

"We need to eat," Pig 789 said.

323 nodded. They both watched the large feeding troughs, which were empty. At some point, food would pour through holes high on the wall. Grains and oats and whatever else. Both pigs, riddled by intense hunger, looked up at the holes in the wall and tried to will food to come pouring out. But nothing happened.

The mass of pigs began to crowd around the troughs, pushing and prodding, anticipating the food, anticipating the holes opening and the subsequent scent of barley and oats, rich and buttery, filling the pen. 323's stomach growled. She pushed with the mass of pigs towards the troughs that lined the back wall. She walked over the grated floor, forgetting her earlier fear of it, forgetting the fact that she was now aware, that things had changed, and also that something was wrong, that the food should be barreling down from its source, its unknown source. It wasn't.

The pigs resorted to their old noises now. The food had always come. It had slid down the feeder shafts at the same time every day. They knew this without knowing they knew it, just as they knew to cram together when the storms attacked the roof of the pen, just as they knew when to relieve themselves or how to chew.

"Something isn't right," 323 said quietly to 789. "I have a bad feeling about this."

"What do you mean?" 789 asked. "What's a bad feeling?"

"I don't know, but I don't feel good. I don't feel like myself. I keep seeing these strange things, images. I don't know from where. But my skin hurts. It feels like it's on fire."

"What's fire?"

"Something that will kill us. All of us." Knowledge, words, thoughts, images filled 323's mind.

But 789 had quit listening to 323's ranting. She was hungry and that was all that concerned her.

323 began breathing heavily. The harsh lights that hung from the ceiling began to blink. Or was that just 323's eyelids? She wanted to be alone. She wanted all the other pigs to leave. She wanted to leave. She could feel the waste on the floor. She could smell its pungent acidity. The smell made her nauseated. The lights flickered more. The pigs, all of them, became, once again, one large entity, a fat pink balloon, a distorted dream. She licked her hoof again, hoping for the same salty satisfaction, but she could only taste the waste and the grime. She knew that those stains on her flesh were markings of something very bad. She noticed that the other pigs had the same stains. And all the stains were the same. They seemed to indicate something, but she didn't know what.

"We have to leave," she whispered to 789. But her voice was hardly audible, all breath and no tone. "We need to leave."

But 789 wasn't listening. She was walking toward the other end of the trough, in search of food or different company.

"We need to leave," 323 said again, but no one heard; the fervor for sustenance was too loud, the echoes of the pigs ricocheting over the pen like babbling arrows.

Her legs began to shake. The light narrowed. The smells and sounds, all of them, the new and the familiar, faded into one small dot, just a few feet before her eyes. She tried to walk toward the dot. Every time she neared it, it moved. Her breathing was now raspy and asthmatic. Her hoof began to slip, and this time, she couldn't stop herself. This time, she fell.

She had no idea how much time had passed when she came to. She remembered falling. And then darkness. Now, the false light of the pen blinded her. When her eyes focused, she could see the other pigs staring down. They whispered in each other's ears. They wondered if she was alive, if she was hurt, if she was insane. Through the murmuring, she looked for 789. She tried to remember if there had been anything to distinguish 789 from the others, but what she remembered most was the small tag pinned to the pig's left ear.

323 rose to her feet. The other pigs backed away. 323 felt as though she was waking up from a dream for the second time. But this time she felt more confident about her awareness. She felt she understood it better.

"We need to eat," 323 said.

The pigs agreed. The feeding troughs were still empty; nothing had come down the chute during her interval in the darkness.

323's mind was racing. She was scanning the pen for clues to a mystery she didn't quite know she needed to solve. She saw it as she had seen it earlier: A square pen, cut in the middle with a pathway, lined with metal fences on either side that kept the pigs in either section locked in. There were no windows except the one atop the front door. Feeding troughs lined the back walls beneath chutes that were supposed to pour grains.

Disappointment filled 323. These four walls were her life. This was all she had to show for her time alive. A small spark of anger began to form somewhere in her empty belly.

"We *need* to eat," she said. The words came out of her with a passion she didn't recognize or understand. Any murmuring that was still trickling among the other pigs stopped.

"We need to eat, which means we need to leave the pen."

The pigs flared in vocal uprising.

"Leave the pen?" they asked.

"What do you mean?" they asked.

"How will we eat? How will we feed?" they asked.

"This is our home," they said.

She understood how they felt. She yearned to feel like them. But she didn't.

"We won't get fed. We can stay here forever but the food will no longer come."

Some of the pigs shouted at her, screamed newly acquired and understood epithets, called her names.

"Yell at me all you want, but the truth is in the empty troughs. The humans have left."

"Humans?" A pig asked, her voice separating itself from the verbal din of the others. She stepped forward. 323 recognized 789.

"789. Yes. Humans."

"When have you seen a human?"

323 felt her cheeks flush. She tried to straighten her legs. She tried to come up with an answer.

"I can't recall. But I know they did this."

323 indicated the pen, the metal fence, the locked-down reality of the pigs' existence.

"Don't think about humans. Think about food. We don't know much about humans. We know what food is. Think about food." 789 spoke calmly. Her words didn't have the passion, the anger that infused 323's speech.

"Then why is there no food?" said another pig. "We've always had food. The day we become aware happens to be the day that the food stops?"

"Aware?" "What we now are."

The pigs understood. But there were more pressing issues.

"Perhaps the humans have fled."

"Why would they flee?" 323 responded. "What have they done?"

But here 323 stopped. What was she arguing for? Or against? She wasn't sure of anything. But she knew she was right. She knew things that she felt she shouldn't know. She also knew there was a time and place to fight for the truth, and this wasn't that time or that place. She knew that somehow, for some reason, her voice was the one that the other pigs had to hear. The other pigs felt the awareness, but some were more aware than others. She looked around at the other pigs, seeking those whose eyes spoke a commonality.

"Let's try to get out," 323 said, "so we can find the food source. Maybe it's broken. We all know the food comes from those chutes near the top of the walls. Perhaps the food is just over those walls."

The other pigs strained to see through the walls. The ones nearest the back wall reared up on their hind legs and tried to push the silver wall down. It didn't fall.

"I think you and I should find a way outside and inspect the situation," 323 said to 789.

"Why should we? Why should we leave the pen?"

"Because we need to eat," 323 said again, but it wasn't what she wanted to say. She wanted to say because we belong out there, we belong in the soggy summer fields and marshes, in the meadows with the summer zephyrs, in the orange autumn, rummaging through a cornfield, staring up at a sickle moon. Images kept pouring into her mind, as they must have been pouring into the others' minds, but her mind was stronger, it was sorting things out, it was leading the others. Perhaps awareness was being doled out differently, she thought, unlike the food, which came equally and joyfully to all.

The food...

The pigs were hungry. The food wasn't coming. They argued over how to get out, how to release themselves from the locked pen. From either side of the aisle, the pigs bantered back and forth. Food had to be found. They had to act.

"We need to climb on top of each other," one pig said.

This seemed feasible when spoken. But it proved a difficult, painful task to accomplish.

"Maybe one of the smaller pigs can squeeze through the open spaces of the gate," another pig offered.

But none of the pigs fit that description.

Still others pleaded, "Wait." The chutes would open. Some lied and said that they remembered times past when this exact thing had occurred, when the chutes offered no food for a time, and then, like magic, the food had come, sweet and robust and plentiful.

And some of the pigs didn't participate in the exchange at all. They stood still, agitated, too confused to take sides. Food, they thought.

While all of this was happening, 323 was watching. First the grated floor, then her body, then the pen, and now she saw the fence. The slats of which ran horizontally to the ground, a new slat every six inches, and were anchored by seven metal poles jutting up from the ground, silver but stained copper with rust, each pole six inches higher than the one below it. Every ten feet or so a vertical pole anchored the horizontal poles.

This is a prison, she thought. And she knew what a prison was. A small, confined place to hold criminals. Was that what they were—criminals? We are pigs, she thought.

She had to know why they were all locked away, what sin they had committed. Part of her was frightened. What kind of monster had she been before the awareness? She lamented the unknown wreckage of her past for one, sad moment.

Then she saw something that forced her out of her mind.

At the end of the fence, near the front door that opened to the outside, and on the other side of the pen, was a gate.

It's a doorway, she thought. Where the humans can enter. That word again, "humans." The word tasted of salt like her hoof, it tasted of bitterness and of something else, too, which, despite all her new words, she couldn't recognize.

I'm too hungry, she thought.

She worked her way through the arguing pigs, through the silent ones, the lying ones, the nervous and anxious ones.

She reached the gate. She studied it. It had hinges. She could sense what these hinges were for. They enabled the gate to be swung open, but only far enough to let something in or out. She saw the latch. The puzzle was beginning to make sense. Unhook the latch. Use the hinges to swing the gate open, then leave the pen.

She walked up to the gate. She sniffed around it. She could smell her brethren on everything, a sharp odor of brine and grease. She gently nudged the gate. It creaked. It moved an inch or two. Then it stopped.

The latch was stopping it.

"What are you doing?" a pig with raccoon circles under her eyes asked her.

"We need to open the gate," she said.

She felt, somehow, that the words meant more than they seemed to. She knew if she could think about just that she would understand their significance. But there wasn't time.

"Help me," she said to the pig next to her. The pig looked at 323 with incredulity.

"Help you?"

"Yes."

323 walked back a few paces. She made eye contact with the pig.

"Don't stare at me," the new pig said. Both pigs averted their eyes from the other.

She then looked behind the pig's eyes, to her ear, and peered at the small placard.

"I need your help, 602. We have to get the gate open. I can't do it without your help."

323 then saw something, a spark in the new pig's eyes. Something switched on inside 602's mind. She understood. She understood that 323 needed her, and why. The two sows nodded in unison, and then they both ran full-force into the iron fence.

And they both winced in pain when the iron fence pushed back.

The racket at the fence caught the attention of the other pigs.

"What are you two doing?"

"We're helping each other open the gate."

The pigs stood silent as the words rang in their ears. Then, as it had come to 602, came understanding.

"If we all charge at the same time, our weight should bear down on the gate," said 156.

"No. It won't. The gate is too strong. We need to remove the latch," said 743. "The latch is the key."

They all thought about this, and 323 felt a warmness enter her body, a feeling of comfort and camaraderie, of spirits bonded by a common goal. Open the gate, and open everything else, and open the truth to what the awareness might mean.

And then a human entered her mind. Perfectly formed. Tall, lean, with a yellowy hide. The warmness left her.

"They're going to kill us," she said calmly.

602 heard her.

"What?"

"The humans are going to kill us."

"There are no humans here."

"There are. They made this. They put us here. This is why we gained awareness. To get out of here. We have to do it now. We have to. Otherwise they will come here and find us and we will perish."

The other pigs heard the panic in her voice.

"She just speaks and speaks," said a pig from the back. It was 789. "She's been trying to scare me, us, all afternoon. Ignore her. She talks about things that don't exist. Ignore her. She's not well. The food will come. It's late. This has happened before."

"No," said 323. "The food is not coming. We will only eat if we get out of here."

"But we never leave here," said 789.

"We've never talked to each other before," said 323.

The other pigs thought this over. Some took 323's side. Some agreed with 789.

The pigs looked at each other, blankly. Moments passed. Then 323 let her mind lead her down a new path. "Fine," she said. "Those who want to stay here with 789 can do so. Those who want to break down the door with me can do so."

The pigs murmured among themselves. They had never before moved in different directions. They always did the same thing at the same time.

"Fine," said 119. "I will join 323."

"I will join 789," said two other pigs.

Soon the pigs had divided into sides. They looked at each other suspiciously, asked each other, do you follow 323? Do you follow 789?

The followers of 789 backed away. 323 waited anxiously for them to object to the escape plan, to argue that if they opened the latch, the food might not come for any of them. But 789's mind did not make the same leaps as 323's.

323 spoke. "Let's knock down the fence."

Half of the pig population now attempted to destroy the latch. They tried to tear it off with their teeth, they tried to butt it off with their heads, but the metal proved resilient. The hunger was becoming pandemic, too much to bear.

Finally, they agreed to charge. They made as straight a line as possible and charged, tons of pig weight pushing against the unwavering metal of the fence. Their first attempt proved futile.

789 and her followers watched. Their hunger was making them uneasy. A few of them broke to help the charge.

The pigs tried again. This attempt also failed.

On their third attempt, the pigs dug in. Pig upon pig pushed and pushed. The fence began to shake.

"Push!"

"Push!"

"Push!"

The fence fell. The clanging of the fallen poles reverberated off the silver walls. Many of the pigs on the other side of the pen followed their lead, and soon, that fence, too, fell to the ground. The pigs were free.

All they had to do now was push through the small door. This was easy. The pigs had found their strength.

Outside, the humidity of the North Carolina summer was thick, but the pigs didn't mind. They felt the air as if for the first time. They breathed it in, laughing, jovial; they ran faster than they had ever imagined they could. They had never run before and their legs were like springs that had been tensed, waiting.

Crows came down from the barn and inspected them. The pigs tried to speak to the black birds but the birds said nothing.

"Let's find that food," 323 said. She turned around to see that some of the followers of 789 had followed her instead. But some of the pigs remained in the pen.

"Why aren't you coming outside?" she asked.

"If we go outside," 789 said, "then we won't be here when the food comes." 789's followers grunted their approval. Their eyes were dark, a strange aggression filling their faces.

For a moment 323 felt fear. Then she realized she was outside, in nature, in a place she had only dreamed of in the dim corners of her imagination. She grunted and stretched, then rolled in the grass, took in a mouthful of dirt, ate a leaf off the ground, and ran in circles until she thought she could catch her own tail.

"Pig," she shouted. "Pig!"

II

DOG

*C*OOPER HAD seen guns before. When he was young,
Peter once took Jessie and Cooper duck hunting in Vermont.
Cooper remembered the maple trees, the streams of ice-cold
water dappled with rocks and debris, the crisp autumn sky, un-
encumbered by the saturated muck of the city. He remembered
crouching low in the reeds near the river's edge, his senses
poised like his tail, Peter's hushed tones telling him to wait,
the tense thrill as the frightened ducks flew from their hiding spots, then the shots, the smoke, the fallen bird, the chase
to find the carcass, the fervent need to have the hunter-green
mess of feathers in his mouth. Jessie, at the camp, cooking fish
caught that morning in the river. Peter, waiting in the shallows,
wearing strange yellow wading boots and a funny hat with attached lures and whistles, for Cooper to bring him the kill.

Now the gun was pointed at him—not as Peter had pointed
it at the duck, confidently, as one might point a compass, but
the way Cooper might hold an unwieldy stick in his mouth:
wavering, unsure.

"You've always hated me."

His talking rattled Carol. Cooper sensed she didn't like it.
It frightened her. It caused the gun to shake more.

"Shut up. Quit talking. Dogs don't talk."

"Drop the gun," Cooper said, trying to change his tone from tense to calm.

"A dog doesn't tell me what to do."

She managed to stop her hand from trembling. She walked slowly towards Cooper. "King bit Sally. Her jugular. She's dead. Just like that."

Cooper knew Sally. One of Carol's best friends. Sally's son had a German shepherd, King, who was often left tethered in the back yard, alone, for hours at a time. Apparently King had joined the revolution quickly. Good for King, he thought.

"Good for King?" Carol said. Cooper realized he hadn't yet learned the art of keeping internal thoughts separate from external words.

"So if King can do that to Sally," Carol continued, "no telling what you can do to me."

Carol snapped the fingers of her free hand, to make Cooper focus on her, and moved a few steps closer. Cooper was looking around, trying to devise an escape route, but he kept returning his eyes to Carol's finger, making sure it didn't squeeze the trigger.

"Bill and Betty Forester lost their eyes. Their cats scratched them out while they were asleep. This is insane. The world is going insane."

"Please, Carol."

"Don't you Carol me!" she said, and then she laughed at what she'd just said. "You don't ever talk to me."

So this is the difference in humans, Cooper thought. Laughter had context. It could change its meaning. Just as a gun could change meanings. With Peter, the gun had signified fun and adventure, sparking in Cooper a primordial call of the wild. But guns could also signify fear, pain. Death.

As Carol lost herself in her laugh, Cooper had a cogent thought: I'm going to die now. He was learning so much, so many things that humans said and did that he had almost, but not quite, grasped before.

He thought of Clio. He hoped she was safe. Then he thought of Jessie. He felt frozen. A part of him wanted to attack Carol, to spring at her and tear at her and make her cower in the corner. Even as he thought this, another part of him urged escape—he felt a chorus of exhortation behind him, in the air, in the world.

He did nothing. He waited. Her finger was avoiding the trigger. Cooper looked closer. She was unsure. Her hands were shaking. She wouldn't look at Cooper; instead her eyes focused on an image just behind and a little above him. Cooper stole a look and saw that she was looking at herself in the reflection of the large glass window. He turned back to face her. She dropped the gun an inch or two, then steadied back to the ready to shoot position. All the while, she kept looking at herself in the glass. She doesn't want to be doing this, Cooper thought. She's not a killer. She knows that.

As Carol fought with her reflection over the question of the trigger, Cooper took a few furtive glances around the room. He saw things he'd seen but never really seen before: the hutch in the corner with the magnolia-covered china displayed behind glass, the freshly cut daisies in the ceramic vase on the oval kitchen table. It had all been a blur before that morning. It had been nothing to ponder, nothing to which he gave a second thought.

"What an utter waste of time," he said.

He looked at Carol, whose hand couldn't stop shaking, and realized he needed to make his move. He could charge her, take a chance that she'd have poor aim with the bullet. But if he did that, he would have to accept the fallout from Jessie. He had no desire to kill anyone in this house. His goal was to escape, to leave the two women alive and healthy, to start the revolution miles from here. Clio was out of the house, and he should be out there too.

He was thinking, thinking, and he realized that he was making a decision, or at least, making a decision by not making one. Or was he? He shut his eyes. Everything was still. He felt calm, ready.

And then a scream cut through the noise in his head, a scream so loud it made him want to howl, to create a louder, larger scream.

It was Jessie. She had come downstairs, barefoot, wrapped in her shawl. Cooper opened his eyes and saw that Carol had turned toward the scream, too.

Both the dog and woman saw Jessie dash across the dining room, yank at the gun and knock it out of Carol's hand. For a moment both humans looked at it, now lying on the floor, oddly inert despite the power it held. Cooper was tempted to retrieve it, but then what would he do with it? He had the gift of awareness. He looked at his paws. The gift didn't come with opposable thumbs.

Jessie solved that problem. Within a second, she was holding the gun like a poisoned rag, by just the tip, limiting her exposure, as if the gun itself was something contagious, communicable.

"For God's sake, Mother. What are you doing?" Jessie asked with forced calm. The screaming was over. She nearly whispered.

Carol couldn't answer, but the look of shock on Carol's face told Jessie everything.

Jessie looked at Cooper.

"I thought you were leaving me." Her tone was hurt, accusatory.

Cooper was still wary of a flying bullet. He had braced himself for it, and now the air felt empty.

"I was," he said. "I thought I was. Carol stopped me. I don't know. I don't want to leave you. You know that."

Carol regained control of her anger. "Jessie, listen to me. Sally's dead. People are being killed right and left. The world is under attack. You don't understand what's going on. It isn't safe."

They all knew who she meant by "it."

"Cooper would never hurt us," Jessie said.

"Yes, he would."

Both humans looked at the dog.

Cooper turned his eyes to the ground. "Why couldn't we just be in Vermont?" he said, finally.

Jessie came to him, knelt over him and petted him. The way that he loved being petted. And yet, inside, he felt those exhortations again—in the air, from the wild. He felt his blood race.

Carol spoke. "They told me the animals are forming bands. Bands of animals that roam the street, looking for those of us who don't know what's happening yet. They know that once we fully grasp what's going on, it's just a matter of time before they're defeated. We have to stay here, until all this is over."

Jessie wasn't listening, Cooper could tell. She laughed. When it was just the two of them, she talked to herself often as she drifted, thinking about something far in the future—where she wanted to live some day—or something buried deep in her past, like why her father had left one morning and never came back. Or, recently, why Peter had also left.

"You always were a daydreamer," Cooper said.

"Am I?" Jessie asked.

"A window starer."

Carol was going to say something, but she stopped herself. Cooper sat down on his haunches.

"You need to go, Cooper," Jessie said. She kept looking outside, at the hill that sloped up at the back of Carol's yard. "You were right upstairs. You can't be here."

"Is that really what you want?"

"You of all people. You of all animals," she said, correcting her error, "You know that I rarely get what I want." She smiled.

Cooper walked up to her and rubbed against her leg.

"Get out of here, Coop."

She pushed him away.

He looked up at her, then back at Carol.

"Okay," he said. And though a bullet hadn't torn through his flesh, hadn't robbed him of his new-found awareness, something in him was dying, something just as necessary as breath.

Jessie walked him to the door. She bent down and smiled, cocking her head like Cooper might have at her the day before. She looked in his eyes, looking for what was new. "I spent the last seven years of my life wishing that you and I could talk to each other. And now that we can, we can't."

"This isn't the end," he said. "I can come back. We'll find each other again. This is just a moment in time."

Jessie's tears flowed. Behind them, Carol was still silent. Cooper put his paw on Jessie's leg. She grabbed at it, held it. The tears made it wet.

"Be safe," she said.

He felt her trembling thigh, and wanted to calm her, as he always did when she was upset.

Now wasn't the time. He had made up his mind. He wanted to talk again, but his words were drowned out by a horrific, high-pitched scream. A second later, the glass in the kitchen doors came smashing to the ground. The house rattled. Carol shrieked.

Standing by the shattered glass, shards still falling casually from the edges of the metal frame, were four raccoons.

"This house is ours," one of them said. Another immediately leapt at Carol's thigh and clawed a deep hole into her flesh, a rivulet of blood pouring out. Carol fell to the ground. The raccoon attacked again, going for her neck.

Jessie now held the gun in her hand. She managed to shoot. She missed the raccoon, yet she stopped him in mid-bite. He looked up, surprised. "You have a gun," he said.

She shot again. This time she hit the animal, who wailed in pain. Then, strangely sympathetic to the raccoon who was dying but who wasn't dead, who was in pain and crying, Jessie shot again, this time killing him. And then she shot again, out of fear, out of determination, out of not knowing what else to do.

"Stop," Cooper said.

The other raccoons had backed off. Their leader ignored Cooper and spoke to Carol. "We know guns. You've used them against us forever. But now we understand them too. You had six bullets. Now you have two. There are three of us left. Where is that great brain of yours that subdues all living creatures?"

The raccoons sprinted toward her. One flew into the air and landed on her shoulders.

Cooper scooted in front of her and attacked the two others. Unlike the rats, they didn't seem too concerned that Cooper fought for the humans. They were at war. No questions were asked. The enemy was obvious, even when the enemy wasn't human.

One of the raccoons bit his left leg, but Cooper bit harder into the raccoon's neck, and swung him from his mouth just as he had the rat earlier that morning, until the body went limp. Cooper dropped him to the floor.

Now it was two against two.

"Get Carol downstairs. Drag her to the basement, then barricade the door."

"Cooper, I can't. I have the gun. You can't shoot it."

"Then I'll drag her. You cover me."

The raccoons attacked once more, this time aiming for Jessie and her gun. Cooper leapt and bit into one of them, causing him to yelp in pain.

Jessie shot the gun twice. Another raccoon was dead.

Only one was left. But there were no more bullets. The last raccoon had circled behind the couch, waiting for an opportunity to strike.

Cooper's strong jaw grabbed at the fabric of Carol's nightgown and scooted her along the linoleum. Jessie followed him, walking backward, keeping her eye on the raccoon.

"We can do this," Cooper whispered.

"We can. Just a few more yards."

Blood from Carol's leg was staining the floor. Cooper's shoulder and legs ached. The door to the basement seemed so much farther than mere yards.

Then came another crash: A coyote had butted her way through the front window, the screen and glass. Small, dangerous, ruthless, she sprinted towards Jessie and Cooper.

She got to Jessie first, but the speed of her approach obstructed her aim, and her open, angry mouth, filled with glistening teeth, missed Jessie's ankle. Jessie managed to kick her off for a moment.

"Focus on the door," Cooper said to both Jessie and to himself. Carol felt too heavy, as if her body had expanded and calcified.

The coyote bared her teeth at Cooper, and the raccoon approached, glaring at Jessie. Cooper dropped Carol's neck to the floor, her head banging against the hard wood, and he twirled around just in time to fend off the coyote. Luckily, she was young, no bigger than Cooper. She circled him for a moment, looking for some vulnerability.

The raccoon was equally impatient, leaping onto Jessie's already wounded shoulder. Jessie grabbed at her, screaming, trying to tear the animal's claws from her body. The raccoon's claws caught in the thick fabric of her shawl, and though they snagged Jessie's flesh, they were helplessly stuck. Jessie wrapped the shawl around the raccoon until the trapped animal's attempts at biting her hands became futile. Then, with intense effort, Jessie tore the raccoon's claws from her shoulder. She screamed, but held tight to the shawl, which was maniacally weaving and bobbing and snarling.

Cooper fended off the coyote's first attack with a ferocious bite to the right leg. The coyote yelped in pain. She retreated for just one moment, but with her adrenaline rushing, she attacked once more. This time she caught Cooper off-guard, and the two animals fell over on their sides, nipping and growling. The coyote's energy was limitless, and so was her anger, but Cooper was fighting for more than himself. Taking a quick look to make sure Jessie had managed to capture the raccoon, Cooper flew at the coyote with such force that he knocked the wind out of her. Seizing the moment, Cooper bit into the coyote's neck, harder than he had ever bitten into anything in his life. The taste overwhelmed him—all that blood and flesh. He dug deeper into the animal's now gaping wound, deeper and deeper until blood had spurted and spilled all over the floor, and all over Carol's weakened body.

The coyote went limp. Cooper let go, and the animal retreated, licking her wounds, whimpering.

Jessie took the thrashing and screaming raccoon, still smothered in the shawl, and hurled her through the holes in the glass door.

Suddenly there was no noise. No violence. Nothing. Jessie and Cooper looked at each other, unsure of what to do. Then, a moment later, another crash. Still one more animal had jumped into the kitchen. There wasn't time to see what it was. Jessie grabbed Carol and, with Cooper, they managed to get to the cellar door, open it, and push Carol inside.

The new animal, hearing the noise, leapt into the living room. It was another coyote, much larger than the last. He glanced around at the death lying everywhere, saw the dog and the woman, and paused, no doubt expecting the dog to kill the human. The pause allowed Cooper and Jessie to rush inside the cellar and slam the door. The coyote jumped after them but the cellar door held against his attacks.

Jessie gathered up her mother by the arms and gently dragged her down the stairs. Carol was now conscious, and moaning. She moaned at each bump until she reached the bottom, where she sat still. Jessie sat next to her, holding her hand.

Cooper followed.

The room was dank, dark, and smelled of mold and neglect.

"What just happened?" Carol asked.

Jessie answered, "Cooper saved our lives."

No one was hurt badly, but they all had wounds. Jessie found an old first-aid kit on a shelf. Carol's leg was in poor shape, but for now, they would have to make do with antiseptic and gauze. Jessie applied as much pressure as her mother could handle.

Then Jessie turned to Cooper, placing antiseptic on his wounds as well. The initial pain caused Cooper to wince.

"It's okay, Coop. It's supposed to sting."

He believed her, but kept looking at the blood and trying to ignore his urge to vomit.

After Jessie attended to her own wounds, Jessie and Cooper further barricaded the door, and Carol lay down on an old blanket Jessie had found. "I'm tired," Carol said. "I'm old. I don't know what's happening. I don't know anything." Her face softened and she closed her eyes. Jessie went to her mother and kissed her cheek, with love—something she hadn't done in a long time. Carol, keeping her eyes closed, smiled a little.

"What should we do now?" Jessie asked.

"Let me look around," Cooper replied. "Are there windows?"

"Just two." Jessie pointed to a couple of small openings near the ceiling, rectangular windows whose old, dusty glass let in almost no light.

"We need to board them up."

"I'll do that," Jessie said, and almost laughed. Who else was going to do it? "There are some boards over in the corner. And I know somewhere there's a hammer and nails."

"I'll check," Cooper said. The basement had three rooms. This one was the largest, and lay just under the living room. It was cluttered with decaying boxes and furniture and memories of several generations that had long left this earth. Under the kitchen was the old boiler room; its rancid smell could repel any mammal. Cooper glanced inside and closed the door.

The final room was another storage room; this one looked as if no one had been inside it for decades. Cooper used his nose to pry the half-rotted wooden door open. He sniffed. Odd, he thought. Something was here that didn't belong. He searched the perimeter. Then he looked up on the various shelves and pegboards. Nothing. He found a closet and pushed open the door with his snout.

There. The unmistakable smell.

Clio.

"Well, would you look at that? You found me." She jumped from the closet shelf and landed softly on the concrete floor.

"What are you doing here?" Cooper asked.

"I was leaving. But the old woman blocked the door. I came down here, looking for an escape."

The two animals watched each other, unsure of the other's motives. A familiar impasse. They had grown up together, in that apartment on Avenue A, and knew each other as well as they knew anyone, anything. They had a fondness for each other. But they did not understand each other.

Cooper's legs suddenly gave way. The wounds, combined with his fatigue, were too much. He slumped to the floor. The cat, concerned, smelled his nose.

He looked at her questioningly.

"Old habits die hard," she said. "I guess I could have said, 'How are you?'"

"I don't know," he said. "I don't know what to do. I can't go out and I can't stay in. I knew my place. I understood it. I was good at what I did. And now I have to give everything up, for something I don't understand, something a part of me doesn't want to understand."

"You've had it easy. Most animals don't. Most animals didn't, I mean."

"You had it easy too."

"Yes. But I know what the others have been through. I don't want that to continue. How selfish of us to rest here because we were the lucky ones who are matched up with kind humans."

"Most humans are kind. You don't kill everyone because a few are bad. Anyway, Jessie has been so good to us. Isn't that all that matters?"

"All that matters is *our* lives? All that matters is what happens to us? What about everyone else? What about the rest of the world?"

"Leave me alone." Cooper sighed.

The cat looked into his helpless eyes. She was relentless. "I'm not blind to love. Jessie loves me and I love her. But does that make up for the animals who've been mistreated? Does that make up for..."

Cooper barked. He couldn't help it. A loud, angry bark. Clio jumped aside.

"Leave me alone," he repeated.

They were both silent. In the background, they could hear Jessie hammering boards over the small windows.

Cooper sighed. "The mammals will be back, won't they?" Clio nodded.

"Then I'm staying. I won't let them kill her." His eyes traveled from Clio's to the ceiling. She followed his gaze, and saw a burst of fright. Jessie had been wrong. There was a very small window in this room too, up by the ceiling, nestled between ancient boxes.

Two sets of eyes peered through the glass. Clio and Cooper saw those eyes, shining red in the dim light. The eyes blinked, slowly, then were gone.

Bear

The bear traversed the forest, stepping gingerly. He could hear the rustling of things above, below, and through the trees. The forest wasn't normally so active. Something was happening, something unusual, but he knew that no animal would be willing to stop and talk to a ravenous bear. The forest was his sovereignty. Being king made him proud, but solitary.

I'm always alone, he thought. He didn't just feel his loneliness now, he thought it. He expressed it. He kicked a rock. He watched the rock twist and turn through the fallen foliage and dust and dirt. Then he kicked another. He sniffed the air, but the smell of war permeated everything and he couldn't locate any food. He decided to go back down to the river and hunt for salmon.

He found the river easily and then headed south, as the other bear had told him to do. He trotted alongside the river's edge, turning his head from the water to the forest and back, watching the water for fish and the forest for something else to eat. Or talk to. He forgot. He was both hungry and curious.

The sun was still high, but fading westward. The bear kept walking and walking until he found what he wanted to find: a ledge above a small waterfall. He went to the ledge and tested it to see if it could handle his weight. Once, when he was young, he had stepped onto such a rocky outgrowth and it had snapped, sending him into the cold river, causing his head to smack against a rock. He had made mistakes, but he never made the same mistake twice.

He walked to the edge and sat down. When the fish made the jump up and over the waterfall, he would be waiting.

Time passed slowly. His mind wandered. He thought of his mother again, the softness of her belly, the tug of her paw, how she was always aware of where he was. She was probably dead.

He felt it. He wondered if she'd be proud of him, sitting on this ledge, a competent hunter. He'd mated with three females who had prowess and power.

I have offspring, he realized. Like so many other things rushing through his head, he'd never thought of that before.

He squinted into the water. He couldn't see anything. Perhaps the river had been overfished. He jumped boldly from the ledge, flopping into the frigid waters below. Normally he would never do this, he would never scare away his prey. But he had to know for sure. He dunked his head below the surface. His intuition was correct.

He waded to the bank. Once out of the water, he shook his body and beads of water whirled around him, a crazy kaleidoscope.

His hunger was becoming a problem. He decided to try his luck in the thicket. Behind the tree line he began to dig and smell and search. He went from bush to tree, back to bush. Anything would do at this point. But the forest was eerily silent. He sharpened his claws on a young pine tree.

At last he heard something,

A shot. It had something to do with war. He decided to investigate. He didn't know why; his need to understand had nothing to do with food. But knowing mattered.

He heard another shot and lumbered towards the sound.

There they were. Two humans. He thought they might be the same two who'd spilled the oil. Now they were wearing bright orange jackets.

Idiots, he thought. They will be easy to track. He laughed at the thought of an orange hare.

Each man had a gun. They were firing at trees. The bear circumvented them until he stood at their backs. He hid, as best he could, behind the trunk of a large tree.

The men were drinking liquid from cans. Probably that horrible poison, thought the bear. They were laughing, putting bullets into the guns. Then they crouched low on the ground and aimed.

Good technique, thought the bear. He wished he could get that low to the ground.

The shots went off. He was closer to the gunshots and the noise was impressive. They were shooting at a sapling. The first man hit it. The second man hit it. The sapling was left bruised and bent. The bear could smell the smoky residue from the shotguns.

Something rustled. He turned. It was a fawn. She wasn't paying attention; her eyes were on the ground, and she seemed confused. The bear watched her.

What was she doing? He was ten feet from her! The bear had never seen a deer walk so close. What was going on?

She looked up. The bear and the fawn locked eyes.

"Oh," she said.

"What are you doing?"

"My family is gone. I can't find them."

"Get out of here. I'm hungry enough to kill you and eat you."

"Who cares?" she said. "I'm going to die anyway. All I am is food." Her ears lay flat against the top of her head. She took a few steps toward the bear. She took a few more. Soon, she was a paw-swipe away. She exposed her neck to him.

"Just get it over with."

"No. This is not how it works."

"Nothing works the way it's supposed to anymore, don't you understand?"

The men fired off a few more rounds. The fawn's ears perked up. She dug at the dirt with her front hooves.

The bear looked up at the sky. Dusk was falling, and he could see the stars scattered over the top of the world.

"It's getting late. It won't be safe. Go find your family." The bear thought to himself, after he'd said it, that he wanted the fawn to leave. To find her family the way he wanted to find his mother and brother. He'd let a hare go and now he was letting a fawn go.

"I told you, they left. I don't know where they went." She looked at the men in orange suits. "I have something to do. Goodbye."

The bear watched the fawn walk right into the sight line of the humans.

"What are you doing?" the bear called to her. But she didn't answer him. He thought perhaps he should stop her, but he didn't.

The bear heard the orange men gasp and then grow still and quiet. The bear crouched as low as he could, imitating the humans. The fawn just stood there. She didn't run. She didn't move. The humans reloaded their guns, aimed, and fired.

The fawn lifted her head just before the shots were fired. She was submitting with dignity.

The shots pummeled her. Her legs buckled, blood splattering the tree behind her. Her black eyes turned blacker. She fell to the forest floor, not fighting death; she took a few last breaths; her ears pricked up, and then they fell. She was dead. The bear felt sadness. Why didn't she just run, he thought.

The two hunters jumped up and down, overjoyed. They touched hands. They touched the cans together and drank them down. They ran to the dead fawn. One of the men pulled out a saw and began cutting at the animal's neck. He sawed off her head. The bear couldn't believe what he was watching.

Have the respect to eat her, he thought. She was there for you. And you take her head? He thought of the bear he had seen before, also missing a head. He shook his own head.

After placing the head into a cooler, the two humans walked into the forest. The bear smelled the air carefully, so that he could track them. Once he had secured their scent, he walked to the fawn's carcass.

He nudged her with his snout. He circled her, nudged her again. Her golden fur, with those faint black spots, was covered with innards and blood. And with holes, the same holes he'd seen in the bear by his childhood den.

So this was what humans do. Kill and take the head. Leave everything else to rot. The bear needed to learn more. He lifted his nose and found the scent. Before he left, he licked the fawn's fur, not to taste the meat but to tell her goodbye.

He caught up with the humans easily. They were loud, their voices ran together. He thought of the wolves baying to each other while he slept in his den. He would like to have heard them at that moment. A pack of wolves, together, howling into the night. He thought he might even be envious of them. Of the group and the beautiful songs that rose out of those enchanted creatures.

He wondered who came first, the bear or the wolf? He stayed a hundred yards behind the humans and the head of the dead fawn.

Before too long, he could smell something, something wonderful. It made his stomach ache. The two humans stopped. The bear stopped too, studying the yellow-orange flickering lights of the fire that rose and fell and seemed to be contingent on the wind. Fire, he knew. He had seen it before, once, but then it was frightening, huge, relentless. This fire was subdued; the humans had tamed it and used it.

From the orange flames, dark grey smoke rose up and filtered away, lost to the sky.

The bear heard a loud zip, and two other humans appeared from a flimsy tent. These humans were different. They were smaller. Females. One of the humans wearing that foolish orange jacket grabbed one of the females and pulled her close. They touched their faces together. The other orange human did the same to the other female.

Something was hanging above the fire. Food—the source of the smell. His mouth watered, drool hanging from his clenched jaw.

The two orange humans took the head of the dead fawn out of the box. The females grimaced and turned away. They rejected it. This made the bear happy. Humans with some sense.

Then all the humans sat in chairs and watched the fire, which was dancing. It crackled. It was mesmerizing. One of the humans rose from his seat and rummaged through a container and brought out a box. Each of the humans took something from the box, then passed it to the next. Once they all held whatever had been in that box, they put it to their mouths and ate it.

Interesting, thought the bear. What was in that box?

After passing the box around again, the four humans rose from their seats. Two of them locked hands, then the other two did the same. The two humans in orange carried a light with them, flashing it toward the forest. They made sounds of joy as they walked into the darkness.

The bear could hear the human sounds for a while, but then he couldn't. Whatever was causing that smell was still hanging precariously over the fire. He rose from his crouch. He stretched his limbs, which had begun to cramp. He was quiet. It always surprised him that he could be so stealthy when he put his mind to it. He sniffed. The smell of war was still present, but he was learning to ignore it.

He walked to the fire. He tried to touch it, but he couldn't. It was the slipperiest salmon yet. And even though he didn't touch it, it hurt. It was too hot. Interesting. Something that was there and not there at the same time.

He sniffed the chairs. The odor that was left behind was loud and synthetic. It reminded the bear of some kind of flower but he couldn't decide which one. Then he found the box. He put his snout in it. When he tried to shake the box off, it wouldn't come off. Using his paws, he pulled it off; small round discs began falling to the forest floor. He sniffed them. Like the scent of the humans, they smelled vaguely familiar. Tangy and acidic. He ate a few. They were dry. He didn't hate them, but he didn't like them.

The humans would leave a perfectly good fawn to rot, but eat these things instead?

He sniffed. That smell again! He was so hungry. He approached the fire, deciding he would just reach over and grab what hung above the flickering. He got on his hind legs, bent over the light and grabbed. He took a bite. Hare. It was the best thing he'd ever tasted.

He should have taken the meat into the forest and eaten it there, but he was a bear, not used to worrying about anything but other bears. He ate the hare with authority. He was lost in bliss. So much so that he didn't hear the humans returning.

He took one final bite of the hare, which was slick, but not slick with poison; it was slick and perfect. Then he looked up and saw four sets of staring human eyes. He could smell their fear. They had stopped their human sounds. He watched them watch him. He threw the hare into the forest and made a note of where it fell. He would finish it later. Now he had a chance to get a closer look at these creatures and their odd ways. He moved toward them, and the orange humans put out their limbs in an attempt to protect the females.

The bear wondered what these humans would taste like. One of the orange men was fumbling with his gun, which must have been the same sort of gun that killed the skinned bear near his cave and the fawn who had wanted to die.

The bear had never thought that these humans would aim that thing at him. But that's exactly what the human in orange was attempting to do. The bear could still smell the faint stench of the powder from when the orange men had killed the fawn. The two females had tears running down their faces

The man in orange made a clicking noise with his gun, and the bear knew it was time to charge.

The human had no chance. The bear was on him in seconds, his half-ton body dwarfing the tiny frame of his would-be assailant. The bear tore at the orange of the man, ripping it off him. Then he swatted the human's neck and face. Blood poured. He thought of the river, its rapids and falls. The gun flew out of the human's hands. The bear stopped his mauling. He turned and saw the other orange man aiming the gun at him.

This one is weaker than the first orange man, the bear thought. Calmly he left the bleeding man, who was groaning and writhing on the dusty earth, to deal with the other human. This one, much to the bear's surprise, fired the contraption. The bullet jetted by his cheek, causing him to wince in pain. The piercing sound hurt his ears, and the bear rose on his hind legs and bellowed from the deepest part of his body. His bellow echoed through the valley, the cliffs, the caves. The weak orange man shot another bullet but he could not hold the contraption steady.

This bullet grazed the bear's side. A mistake.

If you are going to put a hole in me, the bear thought, you'd better do it the first time.

The bear was upon the man before either could blink. He was done swatting. He tore into him with his claws and teeth, daggers and swords, over and over. Soon the orange man was lifeless. The bear turned around. The bleeding man, no longer orange, now more crimson, was running away, stumbling and whining. The females were right behind the fleeing man, making horrendous sounds.

The bear didn't feel like chasing him. He was tired of seeing lifeless things.

He walked back past the fire, which was dimmer and slower now, into the thicket. He sniffed the air until he found his hare. He put it in his mouth, then walked back to the dead human. He watched for signs of life as he finished his dinner. Nothing.

He rummaged more through the human camp. He found some food that tasted sweet. Red balls of flesh. He liked these, very much. He found more boxes of the dry discs. He tore open a box and ate some. A novelty meal. He was overcome by how cluttered the camp was, but he had seen enough animals to know each species had its quirks.

He decided it was time to go. He went to the dead orange man and looked at him.

Poor creature, he thought, surprised.

The bear picked up the human's limp body and began gnawing, lacerating through the skin, the sinew, the veins and arteries, the esophagus. After some time, the head was attached to the body only by a string of bone. The bear raised his paw up and smashed the bones. The head rolled free. The bear gently picked up the head by his teeth and trotted into the dark forest.

He retraced his steps, and before too long, he had found the carcass of the dead fawn. He was surprised she was still in one piece. He placed the head of the orange man where her head should have been. He didn't know why he did this, but it felt right.

Goodbye, friend.

Then he decided to head back to his den to sleep. He was tired, but sated both in his stomach and his mind. He felt he had done what needed to be done.

It seemed the forest was just as bright now, in the night, as it had been during the day. The white stars shone in uncommon abundance and the large white orb, the king of the white lights, seemed almost touchable. Moon, he said, softly, to himself. Sometimes, when it was this low, the bear would climb a tree and reach out his paw and try his best to grab and feel it and see just what it was.

A swarm of moths rushed by, and he reached his head up and ate as many of them as he could. The bear was beginning to understand how complex everything was. The fawn and the flies and the elk and the wolves and the humans. All doing so many different things at once, but always living and then always dying.

As he neared his den, he smelled the sweet nectar of berries. He went to them, picked a few, sat down and slowly ate. It was rare to be able to savor each bite like this. He thought about the humans, and how they had eaten their food with each other. It might be nice to share a meal, however. He and his brother had done that when they were young.

Just as he was beginning to relax, he heard a far-off gunshot. Humans didn't belong in the forest, they didn't know what to do here. Somewhere else, they should go somewhere else. The bear wondered what somewhere else would look like.

He remembered the day he and his brother had stood at the edge of the line, the one his mother had forbade them to cross. But this time his brother did cross it. He moved past the line, then down the rocks, and then, oddly, he kept moving. The bear watched his brother disappear behind some trees. The bear waited for him to return, but he didn't. So the bear went back to his mother and held onto her tight until she swatted him away, and soon he forgot he ever had a brother at all.

Until today. Why had he forgotten? He wanted to play again now, he wanted those days to come back. He wanted to share a meal. He wanted company.

He lifted his head in the air. He couldn't smell his brother. Instead, that scent of war.

Something inside told him to run, to run for the lights of the city, though he wasn't totally sure what a city was. But he decided to trust his instinct.

He took off like a hawk, flying west and into the dense forest. The bear was aware of the ground, its hardness against his weight, its unforgiving resistance. He felt the branches of the trees brush past him and he knew that the trees were smart enough to find a way to burrow into the hardness of the ground.

As he ran, he roared, he bellowed, and pawed through streams and brooks. He felt the earth. He did not stop for fifteen miles. He rested a bit, then took off again, fast as those humans that had rumbled down the snow. He traversed mountain and hill, flatlands and meadows. He had a sense of urgency that was foreign to him. He wasn't curious about anything as he ran; he had one absolute goal and that was to find the war, the battle that had been lingering in his senses. Then he would know what to do.

The path was worn, strewn with debris. Plants had been flattened, branches strewn, as other animals had smelled the same smell, felt the same need, and rushed to the city.

Finally, the scent was so strong that he knew he was near. He slowed to a walk, exhausted. Most of the stars at the top of the world had burned out. The moon was still present, however. He was high on a ridge now, the scent of war below. He could see a clearing through the trees. As he walked toward it, shouts and screams, both animal and human, rose from below the ridge, wafting upwards like that grey-black nothingness that came out of the fire in front of the humans' camp. Something told him to be very careful. He walked into the clearing. There before him, sitting calmly, looking down, was the large black bear he'd met earlier. The black bear didn't turn. He just spoke.

"That word you used before. What was it?"

"War."

"I think I know what it means now."

The bear walked over to the black bear and sat next to him. What he saw below was unlike anything he'd ever witnessed: animals of every ilk—bears, moose, deer, hares, wolves, hawks, mice, badgers, raccoons—attacking humans. The humans matched the animals in number; there were thousands on each side, humans shooting their guns and animals tearing with teeth and claw. They were destroying each other.

"Guns," said the bear.

"Huh?" the black bear said. But then he nodded. "They're amazing, aren't they? The humans," the black bear said.

For a while the two bears just sat, their bodies quiet, their minds restless, remembering the first of their lives, first time siring young, first time a wasp had stung them, the first feed after the winter sleep, until something became obvious.

"It's time to fight," the black bear said.

"It is," the bear replied.

Pig

Outside. A world of new movements, sights, and truths, tickling the skin, irritating it, amusing it. Gusts of cool within the heavy heat. Flits of color. A wayward wind, soft and delicate, then hard and fast. The sun! A yellow ball flung against a brilliant blue backboard. 323 stared at it, and it burned her eyes. She lowered her head, then flipped over so her underbelly could feel that yellow warmth. In a few minutes her belly burned too. Be wary of the sun, she thought.

Other things seemed magical but harmless: green patches of sod and seed that forgave her weight as she trotted upon them, long stretches of field; forests of corn and tobacco stalks; meandering wood fences that portioned one parcel of green from another; the low clouds of a pending storm drifting casually from west to east; the scent of a nearby lake, lazy and tepid; bass hiding among the deeply rooted reeds; ducks calmly commandeering the surface. 323 was among the living. She squinted her eyes and reveled in the glossy veneer of the world. Things teeming and growing, hearts beating.

"Where is the food?" a pig with a brown spot on her snout asked. 323 tore herself away from the world she had just discovered and responded.

"I don't know. We'll look for it."

323 and the others walked along the perimeter of the pen, their old home. Inside the walls were silver, but outside they were the color of dirt. Underneath its eaves, 323 could see where the chutes opened up against large rectangular panels, which were painted beige against the darker brown of the rest of the wall.

"That's where the food enters," she said. "Something must attach to those openings, something that carries the food."

Had she noticed anything out here that might deposit food? She scanned her mind, but came up with nothing.

602 walked up to her with an air of diffidence. "We promised them food if we left the pen." 602's backside was dirty. 323 guessed she had been rolling on the ground.

"I know. It must be out here. It has to come from somewhere."

"I agree. The food must have come down through those slats near the top of the pen."

They broke into four search parties. 421 took a group south, toward the trees and whatever lay beyond. 602 went east, toward the lake and the dragonflies and the buzz of life near the water. Another pig, 861, took a group north, where the fields started. At the very least, she and her group might find food among the spoilage of the crops.

323 was surprised at how easily the leaders took their place in front of the rest of the pigs, and how quickly the others fell behind. She looked back at the pen where dozens of dark beady eyes followed her movements. 789 and her followers. 323 wanted to invite them out into the sun, but maybe she didn't need to. There were fewer of them than before. Slowly they were peeling off, coming outdoors.

She couldn't muse on this for too long. She needed to take her group west, to follow the sun. That sun! How could something feel so good and so bad at the same time?

She walked west, behind the back of the pen, twenty pigs alongside her. She felt safe with her fellows so close, all of them free and curious and mighty.

Behind the pen 323 found an empty dirt lot crisscrossed chaotically with large, strange tracks. She sniffed the dirt for some clue, but smelled something slightly foul, not animal. The group crossed the lot, planting hoofprints alongside those strange tracks. Beyond the lot was a large expanse of grass dotted with yellow wildflowers bending benignly toward the ground. 323 breathed in their subtle fragrance; it was so much nicer than the stench of struggle that permeated the canals of the pen. She let her hooves drag against the grass. Soon, the pigs had crossed the expanse. Beyond it they saw the source not of their food, but of the marks. Three steel objects waited where the grass ebbed into the hard tar of a road. The pigs stopped their pilgrimage at the gravel.

Something about the loose tar, and the heat that emanated off the blackness, spooked the animals. 323 dipped her hoof into the substance. It was hot. She knew that the sun had acted upon it. But otherwise it was harmless.

"It's fine. We can cross."

But the other pigs were engrossed by the steel contraptions, circling them, trying to find signs of life, a scent to trail, something to help them understand what these things might be.

"They look like dead animals," someone said. 323 agreed—animals made of armor that shined in the light.

The pigs circled the objects, again and again. A few brazen pigs butted their heads against the metal sides, softly at first, but their prodding was useless.

"They must be something else. Some sort of storage unit. Or housing project."

Again, 323 couldn't help but form a word. A word she knew the other pigs wouldn't want to hear, a word that the other pigs would deem false, fictitious, fractious: "Human."

"We don't like that word," a pig said.

"I know. But these things that look like beasts are cars. They're human vehicles. Humans exist. They live near here."

"No," said another pig.

The pigs backed onto the grass, giving their hooves relief from the hot tar. 323 wanted to talk more about the humans. But before she could speak, a scream from somewhere near the pen, stopped her—more than a scream, a chorus of screams, rising up into the air, bonding and curdling.

323 and her pigs turned toward the tumult, then raced across the grassy expanse, over the empty lot, back from behind the walls of the pen, through the courtyard they had entered earlier that afternoon, and back to the red barn that stood to the north. And there, in the middle of a circle of concerned pigs, was a single pig, lying on the ground, panting for air, her skin patched with an odd whiteness, her eyes dull and out of focus, her affect listless, her mind turned inward.

"What's wrong with her?" 323 asked.

"We don't know. She was fine. Then she began to breathe heavily. She fell down."

"The same thing happened to me. Inside the pen," 323 reminded them.

"No. You went dark. She is still with us. Look," a pig said.

He was right. The fallen pig was blinking her eye, slowly.

"Maybe she needs water?" 323 suggested.

"We went to the lake and got her some. She hardly lapped at it. She couldn't seem to get her tongue to work."

"Hunger?"

"None of us have eaten. Why wouldn't others have fallen into a similar state?"

The pigs murmured among themselves.

"There has to be a reason for this," 323 said.

"Of course. There is a reason for everything," said a new voice. This voice came from outside the circle, which was now five or six pigs deep.

323 looked up. Had the sun spoken? Was that possibile?

"Over here," the voice said.

323 shifted her eyes from the sky to the window near the apex of the barn. Leaning against the edge of the opened window was a small, two-toned furry mammal, with a pink nose and a long, horizontal body that ended with a furry tail.

"Here!" the animal repeated, so that all the pigs focused their gaze toward the creature. It spoke again in a reedy voice with divergent tones and pitches and inflections.

"Ferret here," he said.

"Pig," 323 responded.

The ferret laughed. "I know what you are. In fact, I think I know more about your kind than you do."

"Why would you say that?"

The ferret stood up and walked out to the middle of the window's ledge.

"Just a hunch. You've been locked in that pen all of your lives. Just about."

"So?" What did this animal know of the pen? He'd never been in one.

"The awareness produces some interesting correlations."

323 felt that was the wrong word, "correlation," but she didn't correct the animal. So many words were flowing through her head, she didn't have time to examine each one. A human drives a car to get to somewhere else. A lock keeps the doors securely closed. When you move west, you move like the sun. 323 tried her best to focus on what was at hand. "Interesting correlations?"

"Yes, such as pigs shouldn't be out in the sun for very long. You don't have the mettle to withstand the heat."

323 sputtered. "Mettle? We have mettle."

The ferret spun around on the ledge. He seemed to be dancing. "You poor tragic beasts. You've had it worse than most. And it's *still* worse for you, even after awareness. Winners win and losers lose."

323 wanted to climb up to the upper level of the barn and tear apart this low-slung fleck of aggravation. "What is your point?"

"Take that pig to the lake. Let her cool herself off in the mud along the banks. She'll be fine. Pigs have done that forever, since before the time of pens."

"Before the time of pens?" A wave of amazement washed through the pigs. But a few of them helped the fallen pig to her feet. They guided her away from the shadow of the barn and down the path to the lake.

"How do you know so much about us?" 323 asked. She took a few steps towards the barn, distancing herself from the rest of the group.

"Because I've been watching pigs for what feels like lifetimes. I've been watching all of the comings and goings from up here, in the safety of the hay." The ferret reached behind him and grabbed a piece of straw, put it in his mouth and twisted it around and around. He danced a bit more. Then he gave out a loud burp.

The sun, sinking, had blurred from yellow to orange. The ferret raised his nose to the rays, enjoying the heat, then continued, commanding the stage that the ledge provided. He recited a brief history lesson to the pigs. The concept of the farm, the animals. He spoke of horses and cows, of milk and honey, of goats and crops, of chickens and eggs. He twirled and pirouetted with both his words and his legs. Now and then, he burped again.

"Why are you telling us all this?" 323 asked him.

"Because you need to know. They have kept you so ignorant, that even the awareness hasn't brought you understanding."

Again, 323 felt the need to defend herself.

"Who is this 'they' you keep speaking of? And how have they kept us from anything?"

The ferret just laughed.

"Quit laughing," 323 demanded, rage rising within. "I said quit laughing or I will make my way up there and stop your laughter myself."

The ferret quieted. He looked down into the eyes of 323.

"Humans."

"I knew it," 323 said quietly.

Then the ferret disappeared behind the veil of darkness that lay just beyond the window. When he returned center-stage, he had lost the piece of straw but gained a silver thimble, which he balanced awkwardly in his paws. He took a quick sip from some liquid inside it.

"You have water?" 323 asked. "Do you have food too? We are very hungry."

The ferret laughed again.

"There is food everywhere. Go to the cornfields and muck around. You'll find enough to satisfy. The humans won't be feeding you anymore."

"They didn't feed us in the first place."

"Yes they did," he said.

323 dug her back hoof into the ground. "You seem to know all about humans. Most of us don't know if we've ever seen one."

"Most of you haven't. They've rigged this place so they have almost no contact with you. At least, those of you who lived in that pen."

323 thought this over. The ferret watched her think, and then suddenly lurched on his hind legs and danced a little jig.

"Stop that," 323 said. "This is serious."

The ferret stopped. He became grave. "All of what you see before you was created by humans." He spread his paws and waved them, as if they themselves were painting the landscape. "Isn't it amazing?"

"Then why do we fear them? Why do we pigs have such fear when we think of them?"

Another little jig, this time less confident. The ferret sang to himself, then turned serious. "I don't like playing the role of teacher."

"Really? I think you do."

The ferret stared down 323. Then he took a swig from his silver thimble. He laughed, and gave out another belch, swaying a bit, then dancing again. "You really don't know anything, do you?"

"We know what we know," was the only thing 323 could think to say.

"How can you gain awareness and still not understand?" The ferret sat down on the ledge. "The truth is, humans can do things to us, to each other, that we can't fathom."

"What type of things?"

"Things," he repeated. "It's why I won't ever leave the farm. Never. I won't join."

"Join? Join what?"

"The revolution. The mammals are attacking. It's why we're the only ones here. The cats and the dogs, they joined in. They chased the humans, and the humans fought back, and things got bad, and the humans fled. The animals who were left went after them. Or maybe they joined the revolution elsewhere."

Something about the word "revolution" congealed into the mind of 323.

"Everyone else is fighting," the ferret said.

"Take us to the fight."

"You don't even understand who and what you'd be fighting against."

"Then show us."

"It doesn't matter. You won't win. We won't win. I don't like playing for losers. Winners win, losers lose."

The ferret drank. He danced around the ledge with a ghost of a partner, tripping over his front feet, catching himself. "Da-da-da, de-de-de," he sang. "Dum-de-dum-dum da." He swung his narrow hips out and back and out and back, a miniature hula.

"Please," 323 said. "We want to understand."

But he no longer seemed interested in the pigs. "Da-da-da, de-de-de..."

"Sir, we need your help," 323 insisted.

The ferret looked at 323 and smiled. And winked. And stopped his dancing.

"A smile and a wink will get you far in life. Remember that." He drained his thimble, then tossed it behind him into the darkness. "I shouldn't do this for you." He leaned out over the ledge, pretending to fall. The pigs gasped. But he pulled himself up just in time.

The ferret disappeared once again into the darkness of the barn. As he did, the pig who had fallen ill returned from the lake with the pigs who had escorted her there. Her color had returned.

323 smiled at her. She tried winking too. "You're okay?" she asked.

"I feel amazing. The mud. We should all go into it and bask. It's like nothing I've ever felt."

323 wondered what the other pigs were doing, the ones who were out there, still searching. Were they too far away to

have heard the cries? What had they discovered? The truth about humans? Some semblance of the truth? The revolution?

The ferret appeared at the opening of the barnyard door. Standing just a few feet tall on the ground, he seemed too small for his big words. And there was something unsettling in his countenance, something 323 felt she'd need to keep a close eye on.

"Follow me," he commanded. The pigs did as they were told.

He led them down a dirt path that wound behind the barn, past the lake and into the first rows of cypress and ironwood trees, their shade offering a much-needed respite from the overbearing heat.

The ferret talked to himself as he led. At first in a whisper, then louder and louder. "But they don't want you, do they? No, no. They don't want anything to do with you. A weasel. Fangs. I'll never forget..."

"Excuse me?" 323 asked, interrupting the ferret's monologue.

"What?"

"Are you feeling well?"

The ferret looked around at the group of pigs. His eyes narrowed. A bit of liquid formed in the corner of each iris.

"I don't want to be doing this. I want to be back up in my corner of the barn."

"Why?"

"Because I don't want to join the battle. Because I don't care who wins."

The ferret almost tripped over his own legs, and then stopped his walking. Shade from the cypress fell upon them. He stood center stage yet again. The pigs waited for him.

"When I was a pup, the boy of the house found me. He was young and so was I. His mother was afraid of my kind, so the boy kept me in the barn. He fed me. He gave me cow's milk, which I disliked but drank anyway. We were friends. But I was wild, or wild enough, and the boy wanted to test that wildness. He would squeeze me hard, grab my tail, put small traces of something noxious in my food. Then he slowly began to know who I was, and what I liked. He stopped testing me. We played together, we grew up together. I spent the day looking forward to his arrival, I was unhappy when he left. Then the boy grew up. He stopped coming to the barn, except when he had a chore. I was invisible to him suddenly. It made me angry. For a while, that anger helped me survive. It gave me a purpose. For a while, that anger was all I needed."

"All you needed to do what?"

The ferret looked at 323, then shifted his gaze to the ground. "I don't know anymore."

The ferret looked so lost and small. 323 felt sorry for him. But then he rubbed his paws together, smiled broadly, and forced out a string of words: "What I'm going to show you is so much worse than a boy ignoring a pet. Excuse my long-windedness."

The ferret turned away and continued walking through the trees. The pigs scavenged for food as they followed him, finding some among the small shrubs and greenery that thrived on the mild forest floor.

But 323 didn't care about food now. She felt herself splintering. The pen, the noises, the need to feed, the sun, all of that felt so distant.

"Does anyone have a drink?" the ferret asked, knowing full well the answer. "And don't say water. Water is for animals."

No one responded.

How could they? No, they couldn't speak now that they saw, each one at nearly the same moment, why the ferret had brought them to this space in the buzzing trees.

The cicadas were humming, the toads were groaning, and that sun was beating down with a heavy hammer on the bones. Bones. They were everywhere. It was hard for the pigs to grasp. The scent of burned flesh permeated the air with a searing sickening stickiness. They saw body parts. Thrown together like dandelion fodder. Some here, some there. They saw a graveyard. Of pigs. Hundreds of pigs. The dead pigs' ears trailing their tags, each marked with three numbers. The pigs walked cautiously among the pigs who'd lost breath. The shock of it, the shock of seeing versions of themselves strewn about this hidden backwoods cemetery stole their ability to speak, stole their ability to do anything other than walk, step-by-step, and stare.

"Humans did this?" The words creaked out of 323 like a minor chord. She waited for a response, for another speech

The ferret simply nodded.

"And if you go fight them, they will do this to each one of you."

323 slumped to the ground, unable to cope. "Humans." She could go no further, no other word would follow. She could only think about the bones in front of her, the torn ears, the bloody hooves, the faceless snouts. Then she let go. She let go, and for the second time in a day, she allowed the darkness to overwhelm her.

Elephant

First, they had to escape the trailer—and before the trainers arrived at the camp. "We're rats in a cage," Nancy said.

"What does that mean?" Joe asked.

"It means we're stuck. We're doomed if we can't find a way out of here."

"Even rats get a slogan. Being a goat is so overwhelmingly thankless," Joe said, adding a bleat for emphasis.

"It's not a positive slogan, Joe. The trainers will know about the revolution. If they get here before we get out, we'll be killed."

Nancy could see the group of humans lounging outside the trailer. A few had gotten up to unload the tent poles, the machinery that would make the nylon rise until it was a fake sky over a fake town of real animals doing fake things.

In the dusky distance the trainers were coming closer.

"They should have fed us by now," Joe said. "I know we have more important matters to deal with. But I'm starving." He sniffed around the trailer floor for some hint of hay.

"Nothing," he whined, then bleated, then looked embarrassed.

"Do that again," Nancy said.

"What?"

"Bleat. Then kick. Make noise."

"Why?"

"Hal has a soft spot for us," Nancy said and then she stopped. She had something of a soft spot for him, too. But she had learned from her first days under the tent that there is nothing more dangerous than a soft spot. "He always has," she continued. "He won't want us to go hungry."

"Then why don't you do it?"

"Because a raging elephant means something different than a whining goat."

"It means a stun gun, doesn't it?" Joe asked.

"This is one instance where being you is better than being me."

Joe composed himself. He bleated to the heavens. He launched himself into the trailer's grated sides. Nancy kept her focus on Hal, but kept throwing Joe furtive glances. He was going at it full force, playing the part of the starving animal with wild aplomb.

Outside, most of the men ignored Joe's histrionics. But not Bill and not Hal.

"Hal, let's at least feed these guys. We can save the trainers time. Save all of us time. Get set up before midnight," Bill said.

"So you're taking the Kid's side, huh?" Hal half-smiled.

Joe kept it up, bleating like a praying revivalist.

"Come on, Hal. Have a heart. That little guy in there hasn't eaten since Omaha."

Hal looked at his watch.

He's gonna bend, thought Nancy.

"I reckon the trainers will be here any minute anyhow. Fine. Go ahead. Get them fed. What the hell. Get them all fed."

Joe and Nancy turned to each other.

"How can they not sense what is so close?" Joe asked.

"They don't have the ability to sense. They believe only what they see," Nancy said.

The men scattered to feed the animals. Nancy watched, her trunk hanging loose and easy in front of her. She understood patience in a way no human did.

"Alrighty, Bill. Go bring me the feed," Hal said. He was standing just outside the door to their trailer. Nancy and Joe glanced at each other as Hal fumbled with the lock.

He unlocked Joe's pen first and began bailing in some fresh hay that Bill had brought in from one of the other trucks. Meanwhile, Bill unlocked Nancy's pen.

He began saying the words that humans say to reassure animals, the words they say when they want to be reassured themselves. Nancy confused humans. Her size made them wary; her docile nature made them comfortable; her size made them wary again; her enormous eyes made them comfortable; the strange, strong appendage made them wary, and so forth. The words, cooing and soft, used to work on her. They worked on that soft spot. They made her feel loved, and they made the humans who murmured them feel safe. Not today. The words meant nothing compared with the action of the bull hook and the isolation of never-ending destinations and the prison of the trailer.

Bill tossed hay, pellets, and acacia-leaf mulch into her feeding trough, checked her water, and then looked Nancy right in the eye. He looked back at her and smiled. He noticed nothing different in her because he didn't have to. She was just another item for him to check off his list. He wouldn't last one hour in the wild, Nancy thought.

She lurched forward and pinned him against the metal grates. She could feel the rough denim and sweat-soaked cotton of his clothes; inside them his bones seemed to melt more than break. Her 9,000 pounds against his 175. She crushed the life out of him. In seconds, he was nothing but skin and marrow. The blood didn't even have time to leave his body.

In the next pen, Joe rammed hard into Hal's body. Hal flew backward, but he was stronger than he looked; those old sinews still had some fight in them. "Damn you," Hal tried to wrestle Joe to the ground, too busy to see what had happened to Bill.

Nancy let the lifeless body lie crumpled on the floor. She turned toward Hal and Joe, who were wrestling and sweating, pulling and tugging, and she swung her trunk hard against Hal's back. She couldn't fit into Joe's small pen, but the damage had been done. Hal writhed in pain in the corner. Joe began kicking up his hind legs, like an angry ass and, with kick after relentless kick, pummeled Hal until the old human quit fighting.

"Let's find the others," Nancy said. She felt odd: She had pangs of guilt about the dead humans. But she shook them off as she might a swarm of flies. She had asked for none of this. "We might need to help them escape."

Nancy stepped into the dusk, a free elephant for the first time since infancy. She let this independence sink in for a moment, and then she surveyed the scene.

She and Joe were the only animals who were free. The others hadn't yet been fed. Humans were jangling keys in front of their respective trailers. The other animals were busy making so much of a racket they drowned out the noises from the pen.

"Let's get them," Joe said.

"No. Wait. Let them free the others first. Patience."

Nancy and Joe backed slowly into the shadows of their trailer. Nancy could smell the rust of death on Bill. Nancy let her body rest against the metal of the trailer. She closed her eyes.

On the voyage from home she had been put to sleep, but upon waking she found herself in a strange land. Gone were the wide open spaces and the plains and the warm air. Strange people watched her with an odd reverence. They watched her stumble down the docks and made appreciative noises. They loaded her up in her first trailer and put a blanket over her.

They drove her to some remote place and put her in a large pen.

At first, she was happy. She was fed. She didn't have to look for water. There were two other elephants with her and the three of them formed a makeshift family. When they weren't in their pen, they were taken for exercise out in the woods, an odd environment, cold. They had taken away her blanket. With the pressing coldness, she wanted to go home, but couldn't remember where home was. She saw a watering hole. She felt the hot sun. And then she remembered her mother. She started crying. No one seemed to care—not even the other elephants. She wondered if they had already cried as much as they could, if crying had lost its meaning for them.

Soon she had her first trainer. The trainer picked Nancy and another elephant called Edgar, who became her friend. The trainer was a woman called Theresa with a fountain of long black hair. She liked to pet Nancy, which Nancy enjoyed. But Theresa wanted Nancy to do things. To take steps this way or that way. And when Nancy, still a child, still newly orphaned, still far away from all she knew, did not move the way she was supposed to move, something stunned her. It tore into her skin with such voracity that Nancy lifted her trunk and shrieked in pain. The bull hook was stuck into Nancy's skin more often than not over the next few months. After Nancy had had too much of the bull hook, Theresa would work on Edgar. The two elephants would take turns learning to do what Theresa wanted them to learn. In moments together, Edgar would rub against Nancy, skin to skin, bonding over the pain of the bull hook and the inanity of the behaviors that Theresa commanded they enact.

When Nancy moved left as Theresa had asked, she was fed and pet. Soon, it seemed the simple choice: Do what Theresa says and be spared the bull hook, be cared for and loved. Why did Theresa give her orders; why did Theresa let the hook hurt her? Nancy had no idea. Neither did Edgar. When Theresa left them alone, the two elephants would stand as close together as was possible, as if the slings and arrows they felt could be alleviated by the other's presence. They snorted and huffed and intertwined their trunks, trying to extinguish the pain. It was only a temporary salve, but Nancy grew fond of Edgar and he grew fond of Nancy.

Then, as the days went forward, Nancy began to get better at the game. She began moving left when asked and right when asked and bending down when asked, despite how much it hurt, despite the fact that she would never have done any of those things back at the watering hole, lapping up liquid next to the crocodiles and snakes.

At night, she was chained to the wall, in a space barely big enough for her to stand. She couldn't move, could hardly breath, and sleep came to her only in desperate spurts. She could hear her friend, Edgar, in the stall next to her, also paralyzed at night by the doings of the day. Edgar, who wasn't good at playing the game, who was stubborn and didn't want to bend down or move to the left, had more bouts with the bull hook than Nancy. They would whisper noises to each other that made them feel less alone.

One morning, Nancy found Edgar was gone. He wasn't there anymore. She knew he wasn't ever coming back.

Later there were other trainers. Some beat her, some pet her, some pet her less, and soon she could stand on her back legs, give children rides, wear the things the humans liked to drape on her. Through it all she was chained and bull hooked, and through it all those trainers were behind her, pushing her, forcing her, then acting like they loved her. Their false praise was what made her most angry now that she understood. They had never loved her.

"Nancy," Joe said.

Nancy snapped back to the present. It was early evening in north Texas. She had just killed a man. The revolution was starting.

"The lion."

And the lion it was.

Both Joe and Nancy felt immense pride as the lion roared.

Two giraffes ran out of a trailer and tore through the tent tops that the humans had started to put in place, stretching their long necks as if they were reaching for high mimosa leaves in the Serengeti. Meanwhile, the lion had torn through three workers.

He roared again.

From the dusty road beyond, the black cars of the trainers appeared and then skidded to a stop.

The baboons came racing from their trailer holding the innards of two workers.

"The other animals are free," Nancy said to Joe.

As the zebras and horses bucked, bowling over men who ran wildly for cover, Nancy saw what she wanted. Fifty yards from the caravan of trailers and semis, and directly south of the half-risen tents, the black cars had stopped. The doors opened and the trainers emerged. They had loaded guns. Yes: It was those trainers, the chain makers, the bull-hook swingers.

"Follow me, Joe."

The trailers and semis formed an arc just north of the half-risen tents. She led Joe behind the trailers and trucks, circumnavigating the battle under the tents, torn down now not just by giraffes but by the baboons, too, who were depositing humans under the big red tops and then suffocating them with their own nylon.

Nancy and Joe ran along the periphery, using the semis and trailers as cover. The trainers were aiming their guns at the other animals.

A baboon grimaced then fell to the ground, his body blanketing one of the humans he'd killed.

The trainers were the worst of all the humans involved. At least to Nancy. It had been easy to blame the drivers and the workers. But she was determined that the trainers, who talked down to the workers, explaining the animals to them as if only they really knew them, would die. And it had been the trainers who made Edgar disappear one morning when the cold was unbearable.

Amid all the screaming, noise, and panic, Nancy and Joe were able to sneak up behind the trainers, who were focusing on the center of the tents, not the periphery. She almost laughed—when had an elephant ever snuck?

"They're mostly afraid of the lion and tiger," Joe whispered, as a large semi blocked them from view.

"Shhh."

Nancy counted the trainers. Three cars. Two from each car. Each trainer had a gun, and each gun was pointed at the lion, who was tearing into a doughy man who had been setting up a ticket booth.

"We need to catch them off-guard, get them all in one round of attack."

"Good plan," Joe said. He glared at the enemy, his odd eyes narrowed. Nancy knew Joe would have proffered those enthusiastic words no matter what she said.

"How do we do that exactly?" Joe asked without moving his visage or opening his eyes.

Nancy wasn't sure. She did know that they only had one chance. Up until this point, the animals had destroyed the humans easily. But, again, the trainers had guns. All six were hiding behind the opened doors of the black sedans. They were aiming their guns at the animals in the distance. They were firing. Nancy didn't turn to see if those shots struck their targets. She didn't want to lose focus on the task at hand.

"How high can you kick?" Nancy asked Joe.

"As high as you need."

Nancy looked down at Joe. He was still posed, statue-like, ready for battle. She looked down. He posed. She looked. Finally, he let his eyes rotate upward to her.

"I know what to do, Nancy."

"Good."

They both took off. Joe's sprint was a prey's spring. Drunk with ambition, he was up ahead of Nancy, bouncing, off to the right in one leap, then off to the left on the next. He stumbled, regained his balance.

Nancy wanted to raise her trunk and trumpet as she charged, but she knew better. She wanted to trumpet her pain, the pain of those years chained, but revenge wasn't a triumphant call to the sky.

Joe reached the first car. The two men were too focused on the animals in front of them to care about, or notice, what was behind them. Joe bucked hard into the first trainer, who lurched forward from the blow, losing the grip on his gun and flinging it forward into a patch of dead grass. The second trainer turned, but Joe had bounced to the right of the open door, swerved backward, and kicked his legs into the trainer's chin. The trainer winced in pain and dropped his gun. Joe grabbed it with his mouth and tossed it as far as he could with a fling of his neck.

The two trainers on the other side of the black sedan aimed their guns at Joe and unloaded. Joe used the car as a shield. But the humans were coming now, converging on Joe, one around the trunk of the car, one around the hood. Joe panicked. He had thought death didn't matter. Now, facing it, he thought it did.

The humans were seconds away when he heard Nancy scream, "Move!"

He lunged forward, near to where he'd flung the gun. Nancy ran at full steam over the black sedan and the two trainers. She wasn't sure if they were dead. She didn't care. They were at least wounded and disarmed.

The trainers in the other black sedan heard the commotion and aimed their guns at Nancy.

Finally she trumpeted.

She charged and they shot. They were too nervous; they weren't quick enough, they weren't accurate. These weren't warriors. These weren't soldiers. Nancy was upon them in seconds.

She took out the first man with her girth. The other, crouching to the side of the car, shot Nancy in the leg. She fell and couldn't rise; her body was strangely contorted, half of it on the crushed car and the other half on the crushed trainer. She couldn't run. Was this death, she wondered?

Nancy looked at her assassin. She wanted him to be Theresa, her first trainer, but no. It was a nameless man.

He aimed the gun. And just as he fired, the lion jumped in front of Nancy. As the bullet tore through his mane, then his muscled neck, as it passed through that neck and out the other side, the lion ripped through the man's jugular, blood bursting forth. The lion chewed his final meal. Then he covered his body with his kill and died.

The circus massacre had ended. The dead littered the field. The tents were deflated, torn like flesh. There were very few animal casualties: the baboon, the lion, and two horses. Others were wounded, but no one badly. Once the animals realized there were no circus folk left to kill, they gathered around Nancy. By this time, she'd managed to rise from the ground by sheer will.

"What do we do now?" a zebra asked.

"We'll figure it out," Nancy said. The pain was bad. But she forced herself to remember the intense pain that had been used to train her, and knew well what she could survive.

"We should go into town. Kill more of them," said the remaining baboon. "They killed my friend."

"I can't do anything right now, because I can't walk," Nancy said calmly.

"I can fix that," said Joe.

Without asking, he began gnawing on her leg.

"Joe?"

He bore into her leg with his prodding tongue. The other animals watched with curiosity. Joe's relentless nature paid off again. After a few more minutes, he found what he was looking for.

The bullet gleamed in his teeth, reflecting the bright lights the humans had begun setting up before the battle.

"A flesh wound," Joe said. "You'll be fine."

"Thank you," she said.

"So we go into town?" the baboon asked again.

"Is everyone accounted for?" Nancy asked. "The living and the dead?"

"Everyone but the tiger. No one can find him. They would have gone after him first," said one of the giraffes. "He's a tiger," she added, and everyone understood.

"I need to rest for the night," Nancy said. "You all can do whatever you'd like. We're free animals now."

"I don't feel free," said a small monkey. "I feel hungry and tired."

"You will feel free in time. It will take time. We should rest."

The animals agreed. They curled up and, only a short while after a frenzy of killing, they relaxed, and they fell into a deep sleep.

Except Nancy. Unlike the monkey, she did feel free. But she didn't feel satisfied. She glanced at the foot of the trainer who had killed the lion.

This foot had never been chained.

This body, though dead, had never been beaten by hooks that tore the flesh.

This was far from over, Nancy realized. She would need to do something more than just kill these humans. The beginnings of various ideas, random and hopeful, like the beginning of freedom, excited her. Joe had curled up next to her, his head resting on her wounded leg, and now he bleated softly in his sleep. She soothed him with her trunk. But even as the other animals snored, wheezed, purred, and moaned in their sleep, Nancy's enormous eyes remained open, looking into the past and the future, hoping that one might make up for the other.

III

PIG

A NEW WORD entered 323's swelling vocabulary. "Death."
A simple word, just one solitary syllable, yet it seemed to be the
most important word 323 could fathom, and the worst word,
too. Worse even than "human." ‘

She shook the darkness out of her head and forced herself
to rise from the ground. She didn't have time to think about
words. She didn't have time to think. She needed to organize
her mind, and then the other pigs. First, she had to make
sure all of them had seen the terrifying sight the ferret had
shown her. This meant sending for the few pigs still standing
with 789 in the pen. These pigs were glad to leave their old
surroundings, having heard the sounds of eating coming from
outside, but when they arrived at the burial heap, their happiness dulled. They took their turns treading carefully through
the mountain of dead pigs, ears pinned down in some show of
primordial respect, their half-closed eyes indicative of the sudden realization that the harrowing scene might have featured
any one of them.

"We feel what they felt," 323 murmured as she rested in the
shade.

A large group of pigs were sitting with her. They twisted blades of grass in their mouths and twitched to rid their backsides of horseflies.

"We can't stand for this," 323 continued. "We have to do more than walk through this graveyard with somber faces and heavy hearts."

Other pigs were speaking in the background, concerned only about food or the lack of food, about heat and mud, but no one listened to them. When 323 spoke, the other pigs expected to hear something of import. Their ears perked up, their faces stilled as they gazed straight at her.

"This is why we're fighting," 323 said. "If we don't fight we end up here, torn apart." She wanted to say more—but no more words formed.

The other pigs nodded agreement. 323 suspected they didn't understand what she'd said, or what the word "fighting" really meant, but the anger that she felt had settled into the others as well, and they were willing to be her army.

The pigs looked at her expectantly and she struggled to continue her speech. Then two pigs approached from the west. "We smell the food," one of them said.

"Where?" 323 asked, and the pig pointed her hoof toward a large cylindrical building, three hundred yards away from the walls of the pen.

She could feel the excitement brewing among her compatriots. But the pigs did not run. 323 forbade this. She demanded order. The pigs marched. They dug their hooves into the earth and made their prints known.

The large door to the building was locked, but it wasn't a match for the relentless energy of dozens of hungry pigs. Within minutes they'd rammed it down and entered the facility. The food was good. It was different. The kernels of corn were whole, not ground up. The oats seemed fresher, more robust. These morsels sat in 323's belly differently than her normal feed. She didn't feel the need to eat more than her fill. So she didn't.

As the rest of the pigs ate within the confines of the silo, 323 sat outside and watched the sun set for the first time. The sight was breathtaking; she understood now why the sun had been one of the first images she was privy to: an orb that rises and descends, that is steady in its properties and has the ability to change, to evolve as the day evolves, to rest when it is time to rest. The sun controlled the day; the sun created the day. As these young thoughts paraded through her mind, she realized that everything she saw outside the pen had not been made by humans. She was learning to discern the difference between humanity and nature. Nature belonged to everyone, but pigs, it seemed, belonged to humans.

She wanted to understand more.

She looked up and silently asked the sun why. But the sun's only answer was to turn a deeper shade of orange.

After the pigs had finished eating, they began to discuss where they might sleep for the night.

"We can always go back to the pen," 861 offered.

"No," 323 said. "We sleep wherever we want. This is our land now. But I for one am not tired. I would like to hunt the humans."

Some agreed with 323. Others wanted sleep. 323 realized that being a pig did not mean being like other pigs. In the pen, a pig was a pig. Out here, each pig was his or her own being. Or perhaps that had always been the case but they just hadn't known it.

Some of the pigs found places to lie down, and some of them began walking. They hunted and explored. Though the sun had finally disappeared, 323 kept walking, kept searching. For what, she did not know.

She closed her eyes and pictured the cemetery.

She thought of herself in that pen.

She thought of the food that was shoveled through the slats in the walls.

She thought of the silo with the stockpiled food.

She kept her eyes closed. The evening hadn't cooled much; the heat was still pervasive, intrusive, liquid. The sun had never really left, she thought. And we are to humans what the grains are to us. Is that all that matters—food? she wondered.

The day was burying itself in night, the cicadas' hum mellowing to a faint lisp, but now 323 saw the wood-framed house, painted white with blue trim, just beyond the tar drive.

"That must be where they live," a pig said. 323 didn't know who said it, but she knew the pig was right.

The group approached the house with a silent reverence. They dropped their heads. They kept their mouths shut.

323 reached the wooden steps that led to the porch. The wood was beginning to rot. She gingerly placed her hoof atop the first step, making sure it could handle her weight. When she deemed it safe, she scurried up the stairs. At the top, she saw a chair with a cushion tied to it, another chair next to it that rocked slightly in the wind. 323 walked toward them, curious. But the commotion of the other pigs caused her to turn around and watch as they scampered up the stairs and filed along the porch, their large pink bodies glowing slightly in the emerging moonlight. Instinctively, many of the pigs sniffed around the floor for the remains of food. They found crumbs everywhere. A waste, 323 thought. Humans ate whenever they wanted to.

"We should go inside," she said. 323 wanted to see how they lived. She wanted to see the inside of their pens.

Yes, the others said.

They looked at the door and once more prepared to ram it down. They charged, but to their dismay discovered that, just as all pigs are not the same, all doors are not the same. This one gave almost no resistance, and the charging pigs were inside the house before they understood what had happened, piled upon each other in the hallway, struggling to right themselves.

323 walked through the opening as the pigs sorted themselves out. As she smelled the air, it occurred to her that perhaps the ferret had been wrong; perhaps the humans were still here.

"Stop!" Her whisper was as loud as a whisper can be and still retain its name.

The pigs stopped.

"*They* might be here," she said.

A couple of the pigs in the back of the pack turned and ran out of the open front door, down the steps, and off into the night, back to the security of the pen.

The rest stayed put. 323 used her snout to guide a few of the braver pigs in different directions, so that they might sniff out any lingering humans.

"Quiet," she said, though no pig now made a sound. "Unless they spot you. Then be loud. Be very loud."

She added the word, "Pig." The pigs lifted their heads a little higher at the sound, fixing looks of determination on their faces, squinting their eyes into focus, then left to search the house.

323 walked into a room that held a large table with chairs arranged around it. Objects that she had never seen before made a strange sense to her. It was as though she could see the humans in the room, using the sofa and reclining chair and cabinets, as if she were watching a movie that was continually

playing all around her. This is where they eat, 323 thought. They sit at this table and food comes to them, not through chutes and tunnels. No, they serve each other food, and they sit here, and they eat it.

The food comes from in here, she thought as she walked into a room filled with shiny metal objects. This was where they prepared their meals. She stared at the sharp utensils, the dishes, things that she had never seen before but whose use she quickly comprehended. There's always food here, she thought, and they eat it all the time.

Then she noticed: fruit. One of the long metal counters supported big bowls of fruit. She could smell fresh apples, plums, pears, and bananas. She eyed it all helplessly. It was out of reach. She looked around. Was there something she could use to jump up onto the counter? There wasn't.

Was this another trick the humans had decided to play on their pigs? It wasn't enough that they had killed the other pigs, that they had kept her and the rest of the pigs trapped behind those iron gates and locked doors. Now they had to dangle fruit just out of reach. She imagined herself tasting the tartness of the red apples, feeling the softness of the ripening bananas in her mouth. We deserve these, she found herself thinking. *I deserve these.*

The sounds of the pigs rummaging upstairs shook her out of her daze. Had they discovered humans? She raised her ears. She wanted the humans to be here, she wanted the pigs to have a chance to charge and attack, to do something other than scavenge and wait and wait longer.

She bent low, readying herself for a charge. But she also watched the fruit, as though it might move, might disappear into the air, as if it might require an attack. Her mouth watered.

She heard nothing alarming. The ferret had been right. The humans had left.

323 knew that staring at the fruit wouldn't bring it to her. Reluctantly, she left the kitchen and met the other pigs as they began to descend the stairs.

"Empty. And no places to sleep. They have beds, but we can't get up on them," 613 said. 613 was smaller and more agile than the other pigs. If she couldn't jump on the beds, none of them could, 323 thought. "I think it would be best to rest wherever we wish outside, to sleep, then wake up early and make our way to the front."

The other pigs agreed.

"But what if they come back in the night?" 323 said. "Someone should stay here."

"Do you think that's wise?" 613 asked.

"I do. And I'll stay."

The other pigs nodded. None of them wanted to remain in the house. 323 watched them disappear into the evening. She was glad to be alone. But she felt guilty. Was she staying to help her kind? Or did she want the fruit? It didn't belong to her alone. But no one else had smelled those amazing fragrances. No one else knew it was there. Why hadn't she told them?

Alone—she realized that this was her first time alone. How strange. She walked through the empty house with careful steps. She instinctively understood some of the objects in the house. The tables and chairs. The utensils and tools she understood too. Humans needed help to eat and sleep and sit. She felt a moment of empathy for them.

She stepped into a room which she knew must be where the adults slept; then she entered other rooms where their progeny surely spent their nights. These beds were smaller;

the clothes that were strewn on the floor were also smaller. A family lived here. Things were becoming clearer and clearer to 323. This was a large home where humans lived together, generations of them, all eating together and sleeping in comfortable beds and having all the time in the world to be with one another. She looked up at the walls, and saw images there: humans. Babies with shocks of blond hair, toddlers with missing teeth and the smiles to prove it, teenagers with acne and awkwardness, poised for first kisses. They seemed wonderful, 323 thought.

She went back into the room where the adults lived. There she saw more pictures—strange that she hadn't seen them the first time. Here were the adults. The humans in these photos lacked the delight of the kids, they lacked the spark. They smiled just as their children had, but there was something forced or reluctant behind those smiles, and yet there was honor in them too. A complicated pride in the smile, a pride in the fact each human was able to find something to smile about. 323 kept walking. She wanted to get away from those photos, from the promise that they held captive. She was tired of looking at human happiness.

At the end of the hallway, she came across a mirror that hung from the floor to the ceiling. She was startled at first to see a facsimile of herself staring back. This wasn't the same as looking at another pig with similar features. She stared into her own eyes with the same intensity she had stared at the photos. But now the eyes stared back, just as intently. She moved in as close as she could to the quicksilver, her breath staining it with fog, and the mirror seemed to move too.

She posed. For a photo. She tilted her head like the babies. She opened her mouth and smiled as broadly as she could.

Her imagination roamed, filling the loneliness of the house, of her mind—with noises and complaints and tussling and joy.

In her mind, babies were crying. She could hear them in the rooms down the hall. "They must be hungry," a pig said to her. The father.

"Yes," responded 323. "I have fruit waiting in the kitchen. Let's let them cry. Just for a little while."

"Sometimes it's good to get it all out," he agreed.

"Father will be home soon, child," 323 said to a boy pig. He was big now, he could feed himself, his crying had ceased years ago. "I made my bed," he said proudly. 323 beamed at him and kissed him atop his pink, glowing head.

"Can you believe she's getting married?" 323 said, stifling a cry. "Now, now, my dear. This is what happens. This is what happened to you and me, and now it's happening to her."

"Oh, I know. But you have to just let me be a silly old pig, with silly old emotions." The young female pig came out of her old room with the knowing glance of a full-grown animal. Her parents, older, gravity winning its war against the sagging belly, beamed with pride.

"I loved you most of all," 323 said as the two old pigs sat on the porch, watching the sunset. He looked over at her and he kissed her gently upon the brow. "You've made this life, these burdens, the sun and the sunburns, seem like jewels."

323 opened her eyes and studied herself. A wave of silliness passed over her. The fantasies drifted away, but they left something within. 323 missed the orbit of the living. She longed for human routines, rising and working and taking pictures and building worlds like this farm. How must it feel then to rest under blankets after the day's toil? She wished she would have

the opportunity to make something of herself, even if all she made was a mess.

"There is nothing to make," she said aloud, into the mirror, into the emptiness of the house. "There is nothing. My life has had no meaning. No reason."

Her body slumped. She felt a range of emotions, but they were all unhappy, despairing. Was this what awareness brought? Maybe it would have been better to stay in the pen, never to know what she now knew, to be born, be fed, to sleep, and to die without knowing anything else. Ever.

She could barely walk now. Each time she lifted her hoof, she held it in the air for as long as she could, thinking about the next step. She closed her eyes. The next step, the next step. Her mind raced. She pictured a million steps in an endless meadow, her hoof planting itself again and again in the soft ground, an endless messy line showing only that she once took another step, that she once walked, that she once was. And then she watched the hoofmarks disappearing, washed over by the rain and the sun, washed over by the markings of other animals, maybe humans—bigger, stronger, faster animals, until the proof she had stepped was gone forever.

She put her hoof down; it made a gentle thud.

She gazed at herself. Her eyes closed and then opened.

"Pig," she said, and then walked away from the mirror and down the stairs.

Sleeping in the pen would be fine. She belonged there.

As she trudged down the stairs, she heard a noise in the kitchen.

She tensed.

Had they come back? The humans?

Another noise.

Did she care? Maybe it was somehow right that the humans kill her, right here, in their house. Why not? They were probably going to take her anyway, someday, somehow. Might as well get it over with. Suddenly death seemed like a welcome friend.

She scraped along the edge of the wall. When she finally reached the bottom of the stairs, she turned to walk through the dining room and into the kitchen.

"Oh, well, looky, looky, looky," 323 heard as she passed through the dining room. "I have stashes upon stashes upon stashes."

323 peaked her head in through the kitchen door. There, upon the counter, was the ferret. He was doing his dance, singing his song. "Da-da-da, de-de-de, dum-de-dum-dum da." He misstepped, fell on the counter, and looked up self-consciously to see if anyone had been watching.

"Oh my, a pig," he said.

Then he tore a banana from a large bunch in the fruit basket. He peeled it with carefully with his mouth, and then tossed the fruit to the ground.

323 looked at the banana. Once again, she could almost taste it. But this time she opened her mouth and she did taste it.

"Is it good?" the ferret asked.

"Yes," 323 said between swallows.

"It seems only fair that you eat *their* food," he said.

"I'm too tired to play your games. Once was enough."

"No, no. It wasn't enough. Look at you. A dark, dark pig. With dark, dark thoughts. Don't think I didn't hear you."

"Leave me alone. Or, perhaps, give me an apple, and then leave me alone."

"Get your own apple," the ferret said. He hopped around, showing off his nimble steps. Then he fell again, and burped, and laughed. He threw an apple at 323 and it bounced off her brow. Then, without saying a word, the ferret took off upstairs, giggling, leaving 323 alone in the kitchen.

"It's not as good as I thought it'd be," she said after she ate the apple.

"It should be better. Forbidden fruit," the ferret said. Just like that, he had returned from whatever mission he had sent himself on.

"Where'd you go?"

"Here and there," he said, still laughing.

323 smelled something in the air, something foul. The ferret had brought the stink of humans back into the room.

"Like I said, I'm too tired for you. This day. It hasn't been what I'd hoped."

"And what did you hope for?"

"It doesn't matter."

He tossed her a plum.

"Try this one instead."

She didn't want to try anything, but she couldn't help herself. The plum was delicious—so sweet, so cold. She hoped the other pigs would forgive her as she ate what they had never tasted.

The ferret took a drink from his thimble. He burped once more. Then he winked.

"I see you."

"Of course you can see me."

"No, I see inside you."

For a moment 323 felt naked, vulnerable. But the ferret was probably just talking nonsense. She finished off the plum and wished for another.

"You've seen what you've seen. You know truth. Truth hurts. A lot. We're all finding that out."

"Stop talking," the pig said.

"Poor unhappy pig. Poor unhappy pig. Da-da-da-da-da-da. Well, sitting around being unhappy isn't going to help anyone."

"I don't want to help anyone."

"Yes, you do."

"No, I don't."

"Fine. You want to be like me? Here, drink." He jumped off the counter and rushed towards 323. He put the liquid under her nose. She sniffed it and drew back. The ferret nodded.

"Follow me. Who knows how much time we have, who knows if we have any time at all."

"Time for what?"

"You don't want to be like me, pig. I see something in you. Something I wish I saw in me. But it's not there. I know that. It's been gone for as long as I've been strong. No. The opposite. Never mind. So, come with me. Or drink. That's the choice. Up to you."

The ferret scampered toward the open front door. He paused and turned, waiting for 323 to decide.

"You come with me," the ferret said, "and your world will never be the same. You won't be the same."

323 rolled this promise around in her mind. She had already seen the burial ground. She had seen the human home. And she was ready to give up on this world that existed outside the pen. There was nothing to do, there was nothing more to learn except misery. At first she thought, Why bother? Why did all this have to happen?

Oddly, and not for the first time, the ferret seemed to understand what she was thinking.

"Come with me." He said it with such conviction that she knew whatever she was about to see would turn her world upside down again—so many times the world was turning and turning! She was turning too. Her body was turning, following. Even though she still felt glum and moody, she was putting one hoof in front of the other, and once again taking slow, unwanted steps toward her fate.

Elephant

The animals spent the night circled around the crushed car as if it were a campfire. The gentle hum of sleeping diminished the aura of violence, and, although carcasses scattered the fields like fleshy weeds, this was a peaceful evening. Predator and prey slept as one, breathing in and out, over and over, in and out.

The issue of hunter living beside the hunted had been resolved quickly. Of all the animals in the circus, only the lion, who was dead, and the tiger, who was missing, might eat the others. The rest were omnivores or herbivores, which meant they competed with each other for food rather than acting as food for each other. For now, Nancy thought. She wondered about the tiger, but hoped, if he were still nearby, that the human bodies would tide him over.

The tiger was just one of many concerns that kept Nancy awake. She kept replaying the events of the afternoon. What could she have done differently? Four of her kind had been killed. She wanted to bury the lion and honor him somehow. She wanted him to come back to life so she could thank him. Most of all, she wanted him to be the leader, so that she could sleep like everyone else. She wanted to forget. She wanted to stay awake and think. She didn't know what she wanted.

The sun rose over an eastern butte, and an edgeless pink overtook the sky. Nancy watched the world with new eyes. It looked beautiful.

She flexed her leg. It felt better than it had even a few hours earlier. Whatever Joe had done, his little goat mouth digging at her rough skin, seemed to have worked.

Nancy knew that Joe and the others would expect her to have a plan. In the absence of the lion and the tiger, she was the leader.

Images, ideas, worries flooded her mind. The animals needed to leave the circus site. They needed food. They needed water. When they awoke, they would need to scavenge the trucks for anything to drink or eat, first thing. Every plan began with a first step and she had hers. So she watched the sky as it turned from pink to light orange, she felt her eyes become heavy, and closed them, and rested.

She didn't sleep long. The little monkey woke her, dancing on the crown of her head. She raised her trunk instinctively and tried to shoo him off. He was too quick.

"We're hungry, we're hungry," the monkey said. "Hungry."

Nancy rose. The other animals were up. Twenty-eight eyeballs, all trained on hers.

She sighed. "We need to get up and moving. Let's scavenge through the food trucks and find the stored feed and water. They had to have enough to last us many days."

She looked at the monkey, who looked at his hands, and understood. The thumbs. Only he could manage locks and handles. The remaining baboon was too busy weeping for his friend. The monkey scurried off.

"I'll follow, make sure he doesn't get into trouble," Joe said. Nancy nodded. The monkey was known for mischief. But he was also very clever, and he found the way into the food truck rather quickly. He shrieked gently, with pleasure and pride, as it opened. Nancy ambled over to it gingerly and, with Joe's help, dispensed the oats and grains. The animals ate with voracious intent. The killing had left them hungry. Nancy nibbled on acacia leaves, but her appetite was small. Too much in her mind to leave room in her stomach, she thought.

Nancy had the monkey search for the water truck. He found it, and the animals lapped up the water just as the sun was taking every color but blue from the sky.

Fed and quenched, the animals met back at the crushed car and waited for Nancy. She drank her fill and then sprayed some of the water over her back, cooling it off.

As she returned, the flash returned. Something about that water drenching her back, the sun, the heat, this group of kin—caged kin, not kin from birth—reminded her of something. She'd been with a group like this before. She shook it off. These flashes had to stop. Craziness, insanity. These were human constructs, but now she understood them well enough to fear them.

"What now?" Joe asked.

"We have food and water here—but not as much as I'd hoped. There's less than a full supply. This isn't a good place for us. Not with the dead."

"We can join the fight," one of the horses said.

"If there are any real battles near us. I'd guess we're far away. We drove on that small highway for miles and miles since last we saw a city."

"Maybe one will find us as we migrate," a zebra said.

"Maybe," Nancy said. She was distracted by that word, "migrate." It felt right to be out here, to migrate, rather than being in the back of a trailer, trapped by metal; it felt right to be walking toward the horizon, instead of trying to find it from inside a cage.

"Something will find us. Of that I'm sure." Happiness overwhelmed her. The part of her that was animal and the newly acquired part that was aware seemed to be fusing together. It was time to migrate, she told herself, and the sun felt good as it beat down on her. They would find food, they would find adventure, they would find life.

But first they had work to do. "There might be extra food anywhere. Look for whatever you can find," Nancy said.

The animals did as they were told, searching the trailers, the cars, the pens. They found nothing, except in one pen, where something peculiar cowered in the corner. Joe and the monkey approached, and made out a shivering beast, crouching in the dark.

The tiger.

Joe bleated loudly. The monkey clapped like a drunken goon. They had momentarily forgotten their new voices.

Nancy and the others, hearing the commotion, rushed to the trailer and peered inside. Nancy couldn't believe what she saw: a tiger who seemed afraid of the light.

"What should we do?" Joe whispered. He was wary of the animal, as were the others.

Nancy could see the whites of the tiger's eyes, but, no, white was the wrong color. Rivulets of red crisscrossed the whiteness. "Leave me with him," she said.

"Is that safe?" Joe asked.

"I think it is. Elephants and tigers aren't enemies."

"It must be so easy to be you," Joe lamented yet again. But he did as he was told, leading the others back to the comfort of the crushed black sedan.

Nancy waited for the last animal to clear, then poked her head into the tiger's pen.

"How are you, friend?"

The tiger tried to find a deeper corner.

"You can come out now. Do you know what happened? Are you aware?"

"Yes," he said with a meek growl. "I'm aware."

"Would you like to come out?"

"I would prefer not to. You all go and find more of them to hunt and kill, and leave me alone."

"And you'll just stay here? Alone?"

"I was made to be alone."

"But things have changed."

"No. They haven't."

"We need you."

"No, you don't."

"We do. The lion is dead. Shot by a trainer as he saved me. They all want me to lead. But you should lead. You were born to lead."

"I was born to do lots of things I no longer do. I just want to sit here in the dark and be left alone."

"We will be hungry soon and we need an expert hunter."

"There are plenty of dead humans to eat."

"They taste like rubber, the omnivores tell me. Most would rather go hungry."

"Wait until they get hungry enough. They will feast on human flesh."

Nancy paused. "Is there anything I can do to get you to come out and join us? I'm asking selfishly. They are all looking to me to answer their questions."

"Well, you should have thought of that before you destroyed the humans."

"Are you on the side of the humans?"

"I'm on the side of reality."

"What does that mean?"

"They provided for us. They fed us. We get proper thought for one day and we misuse it. Just like them. What did you think would happen with them gone? Food would just appear? Water would fall from the sky?"

Nancy was getting angry. But then she thought of Theresa, her first trainer, of the bull hook and the chains. She sensed the tiger had his own Theresa.

"What did they do to you?"

"Who?"

"The trainers. How bad was it?" Her voice had softened to a maternal whisper. The tiger shifted uncomfortably in the corner. Nancy continued, "You know what they did to me? The kept me locked up in a place so tight I couldn't even raise my trunk. They thought my skin was rough because it looks rough, but it's as sensitive as theirs. So when they pierced my skin with the hook—because I went the wrong way, because I was exhausted from overwork and lack of sleep—it stung for days. And when they humiliated me, laughed at me, thinking I didn't know what was happening, when they shoved me this way or that, I began losing myself. It happened so slowly, I had no idea."

She paused, for though she'd thought of all this earlier, saying it aloud gave it a weight, a conviction, that she hadn't anticipated.

"So what did they do to you?"

The tiger crawled from his corner. He hung his head low, and inched toward her. He was large, but gaunt.

"It doesn't matter what they did. And you'll never hear about it anyway. Not you, not anyone else."

"They killed my best friend. A beautiful elephant named Edgar, because he wouldn't bend," Nancy said.

The tiger waited for her to continue, but she couldn't. The tiger saw the sadness in her eyes and heard the struggle in her voice. He considered his options, and realized he had only one. "I'll come along with you," he said. "Just leave me alone. Let me be."

There was something magical about the tiger. He was a living myth, but a dangerous one. The other animals would need assurance that the tiger was on their side. For many, he was an enemy.

"I have to be clear. Are you with us?"

With a graceful leap, the tiger landed on the dirt next to Nancy.

"Yes. I said yes. I meant yes." The tiger almost smiled, and added, "The zebras will be safe."

"Is that a promise?"

"Consider it a promise."

An hour later, the migration had begun. Nancy led the brigade, with Joe next to her. The baboons followed, then the horses and zebras, then the sheep and the giraffes. The monkey rode on the back of one of the giraffes, eyeing the tiger curiously as he stalked the group a hundred yards or so behind. There, but not there—with them, but not with them.

In the beginning, Nancy kept turning around to make sure he was near, and to make sure the zebras were untouched. But before long, she stopped turning. The road had captured her imagination, and now it asked for her undivided attention.

With each step she was getting further and further away from the circus, and further and further away from her past. The Texas summer, the bee blossoms dotting the dirt, sod and tufts of wilting grass, the aridness—it all felt so comfortable to her.

Joe lagged behind Nancy, then sprinted a few yards ahead, only to quickly lose her pace and lag behind yet again. Now a kick of dust flared up as he dashed over a patch of loose dirt.

The dust stuck in her eyes and as she tried to blink it out, a grey elephant appeared, a baby, playing with her, racing her, beckoning her to come and join him. Nancy found herself racing toward the young grey calf, suddenly desperate to join him. She sprinted, not feeling the pain from her bullet wound shoot up her leg.

"I'm coming," she said. But the calf was losing his greyness. He was turning black, he was turning into shadow.

"I'm coming!" The shadow, black and twisting, started to get smaller.

Nancy extended her trunk, trying to grab the shadow that seemed so intent on evaporating. She grabbed a bit of it and brought it to her, but it was slippery, squirmy.

"Nancy?" Joe said.

Nancy, still blinking her eyes, finally got the dust out.

Joe was wrapped in her trunk, suspended six feet in the air, turned upside down.

"Please set me down?"

Nancy shook her head, dazed.

"Of course, Joe," she said, regaining her wits. "I'm sorry. I don't know what just happened."

"We need to get you some water."

"Yes, I need water," she said, but no, she had drunk plenty. Still, she would take Joe's alibi. She glanced around to see if any of the other animals had seen her pick up Joe. They had.

"We need to find water. It's been a long time since any of us were on our own. Thirst must be quenched."

The others nodded.

Nancy carried on leading the charge, Joe running alongside. The others walked behind her. The tiger skulked in the background. And the bee blossoms were still guiding them towards something miraculous, the blossoms' white petals like grounded doves. Yes, this meant more walking, more one-foot-in-front-of-the-other, but the sky was blue and the metal cages and bars belonged to yesterday.

At noon, they came across a large redbud tree. It stood by itself in the middle of the dryness.

"Let's rest under the tree," Nancy suggested.

Soon, the monkey was playing on the branches that forked off like a tributary from the main trunk, swinging and screeching. The giraffes picked at the soft pink leaves, but they didn't like their stinging tartness. The baboon scratched his back along the rough bark. The sheep grazed on small spurts of grass that struggled to life under the canopy of shade.

Nancy looked back and spied the tiger, an orange blur far to the side of the group. She could just picture his agitated tail, flapping back and forth, waiting for something she couldn't know.

"Can you sense water?" Joe asked.

"It's near. This tree wouldn't be here without water."

Joe leaned in close and whispered, "I know you, and I know you need water."

"I'll be fine, friend. And we will find water soon."

"Can we take a nap?" a bashful sheep asked. Her words were shaky; she hadn't mastered this new speech yet. Nancy sensed she'd been wanting to ask this for some time but that it had taken a few miles before she could muster the courage.

"It is midday. What do you all think?" Nancy asked the group.

A resounding yes.

So they settled comfortably under the redbud tree, closed their eyes, and fell asleep. This time, even Nancy's eyes fell quickly shut.

And this time, she dreamed.

Of a single tree on an empty savannah.

An abstract version of herself ballooned up. She was light, bouncing along the heather and acacia grass, small wildebeests snaking through the tall underbrush, trying to bite her, to puncture her balloon body, let the helium escape, but their bites never took. She found herself on top of a tree, sitting and watching the expanse that lay like an artist's tableau before her. She could see everything. Endless animal footprints in the dirt path that cut a swath among the amber fields. A cheetah sat and watched for prey on top of a mound of dirt. Meerkats sniffed the air for danger and possibility. African buffalo danced clumsily along the edges of a watering hole as sinister eyes tracked them from just below the water's surface.

And then, she saw the grey calf again. He was older now. Another elephant was standing near him. The calf was leading her to the watering hole. Behind them more elephants followed. The balloon version of Nancy felt compelled to go to them, to drink the water with them. But she couldn't leave her perch. She was stuck to the tree. For a second, her dream-self considered how odd it was for an elephant to be in a tree, but she didn't question her situation for too long. She was afraid to move, knowing that the thorny edges of the leaves and branches would do what the wildebeests couldn't. She would be punctured. She would deflate. She made small, deliberate movements, but with each attempt to free herself, she could feel her body tear. So she stayed still as the sun set, as the far-away elephants drank from the watering hole and then left. This time her grey friend didn't disappear into shadow; he disappeared into that horizon....

Nancy awoke, startled. She'd often woken up feeling odd, as though the night had taken her places far-off and remote, but she'd never understood that these feelings, these places, existed within her.

She looked up at the redbud tree, at the monkey sleeping high in its branches.

"Now we really do need to find water." She knew it was crazy, but she thought maybe, just maybe, if they found water, and quickly, she might see him, that grey calf, who was now full grown, and the two of them would lap up the water together. Maybe, if she kept going this way, she would find everything she had dreamed about, just over the next hill.

"Joe," Nancy said urgently, "Joe, wake everyone up, we've been resting for too long. We need to find water."

Joe was slow to wake, but once he did, he commanded the group to open their eyes and prepare for the migration to continue.

Then, as the animals stretched and yawned, as they dragged the final vestiges of sleep out of their minds and bodies, they began to walk.

A few hundred yards from the redbud tree, the circus animals walked into another collective of animals heading east. For Nancy this meeting seemed like an extension of her dream. These animals were strange, each one odder than the next. Most were short, barely reaching the place where the bullet had entered her lower leg.

"Are you aware?" asked one of the animals, who, despite his physical repugnance, spoke with strength and dignity. "Do you have a leader?"

"We are and she is," Joe answered, using his small horns to indicate Nancy.

"Why aren't you fighting in the battles?" another of the new animals asked. Nancy recognized this one—a black and white, bushy-tailed skunk.

"We could ask the same of you," Nancy said defensively.

"We have been fighting. We were in the battle at Lubbock, but we've decided to come east to the next town and see if we can fight somewhere else," said the first animal, with the voice of paved gravel.

"I'm sorry. I don't know who you are," said Nancy. The animal looked like a pig, but a deep brown one, more boar-like, with a rodent-like quality as well.

"How would you know who I am? I am from south Texas and I doubt that's where you're from."

"What I meant was I don't know what you are."

The animal grunted haughtily. "I'm a peccary and I don't like strangers. Life works better for me if I keep to myself. But those days are long over. So here I am, out in the open."

"Well, it's a pleasure to meet you."

"Is it?" the peccary scoffed. "That would be a first."

He then introduced the rest of his ragtag group: their predator, a jaguarundi, looking more like a puffed-up weasel than any of his big cat cousins. He, like the tiger, stood off to the side; an antelope with strange, twisting horns that looked more like prongs than goring devices; three possums, who bore their teeth and poised their claws for attack; and, sleeping on the head of the antelope, using the prong-shaped antlers as a makeshift bed, a ringtail cat, who looked like a runty raccoon. He was their night watcher.

The two groups intermingled for a bit, honoring their old instincts by sniffing and eyeing each other, then gradually using their newfound cognition to get better acquainted.

"So, how was the Battle at Lubbock?" Nancy asked the peccary.

"It was tough. We lost many of our own."

The circus animals hung their heads in tribute.

"Peccary, is there water to the west?"

"There is, but you should join us and head east. We could use a collective like yours."

Nancy considered this proposition. These animals knew this land, and could guide her group through the foreign terrain, lead them to food and water and shelter.

But the grey elephant from her dream had set out to the west from the watering hole, and something about the west still called to Nancy with a power she couldn't resist.

"We'll take our chances in the other direction," she said.

The peccary scoffed.

"There is nothing there but skinny coyotes, slow armadillos, and desert field mice. They have nothing to offer. They are fighting in circles."

"Isn't that all the more reason to join them?"

The antelope with the deformed antlers chimed in. "You don't understand. They won't have you join them. They want to do everything their own way. Even if that means losing."

Nancy looked down at Joe, who cocked his head like a muddled puppy.

The antelope continued, "The eight of us know how to defeat humans. We've been watching them quietly and secretly under the camouflage of night. So when we saw that our more common brethren were losing, we came out of the shadows to help. It worked while they listened to us. Now we want to find others who appreciate our value."

"It's no use," said the ringtail cat with a sleepy yawn. "The elephant has made up her mind." Then she repositioned herself among the antlers and fell back asleep.

"The cat is right," said Nancy. "I want to go west. But join us. We could use each of you."

The peccary smiled. "No, we are done with the west. But you go ahead, if that's what's calling to you. We wish you the best."

The ugly creatures began to leave, walking slowly toward the next battle. The peccary turned around. "The watering hole is less than half a day's walk to the southwest."

"Thank you."

The peccary nodded, then turned back around and walked off.

Nancy and the others walked the rest of the day. The landscape softened, the vegetation mutating from the endless yellow to a smattering of green. The giraffes grazed on the cottonwoods and red berry junipers, which were more and more frequent. The monkey screeched and hollered as he swung from the broad shin oaks and the arching black willows. Joe and the sheep took bites of grass, chewing slowly, to the rhythm of their walking.

Overhead, Nancy spied the soaring blackbird's spreading wings, and she took this image as a sign that she was headed in the right direction. But then a noise disturbed her. A flash. She was back in Africa. She was looking at the grey calf, now fully grown. The elephant whom he'd led to the watering hole was in pain. Her elephant, the calf-turned-bull, the one she so wanted to meet, was pacing around the ailing cow. The noise grew louder and louder. It was deafening. The other elephants in the group, also cows, looked around. The sound shot through their ears. The bull elephant led the cow away. The other elephants followed, but the noise didn't relent. It got stronger and stronger. It was getting nearer.

Run, thought Nancy. Get out of there.

Run.

"Run!" she shouted. "Run for cover, run for somewhere, run to where the noise can't find you!"

"We are running!" Joe said.

And he was, and so were the other circus animals. So, too, was Nancy, though she didn't remember starting her sprint. The noise from her daydream was real. It was coming from the sky. She looked up. A human plane had replaced the blackbird, a crop duster. It was directly behind them, racing through the sky toward them. The pilot had spotted them and was closing in. He was aiming a rifle at the collective.

"He's got a gun," said Nancy, losing her breath.

"We know. He hit one of the sheep on his first pass."

The man in the crop duster shot and missed, then swooped past the running animals, looping a big U-turn to have another go.

Nancy knew the shooter wouldn't miss next time. She looked at the terrain ahead. No natural hiding place. She looked up. The plane had nearly doubled back.

"Split up. Every one of you run in a different direction. He can only go after one of us!"

"And what if he chooses us?" asked the giraffes. "We're the easiest targets."

"Just run. Find trees. Find rocks. We are only an army of fifteen."

"Thirteen," Joe said.

"Do as I say."

The animals did. Thirteen different directions. A minute later, when the crop duster made its pass, it did go after one of the giraffes. But it missed. The plane was being buffeted by high winds above; the bullets went astray. Two more passes yielded the same fruitless results. The plane then flew off to the west. Nancy had never been more relieved to hear the silence of dusk.

Once they realized the plane was gone, the group, shaky and weak, met Nancy.

The surviving sheep were especially shaken. The dead sheep was the one who'd asked for the nap earlier that morning. Those were her final words.

"We should have gone with the other group. They were ugly, but they knew what they were talking about," said the sheep, in angry defiance of Nancy's authority.

"No one stopped you."

"You stopped us," the sheep said. "You wanted to go west. We don't even know which way west is. We just followed you."

"No one asked you to."

"It feels like you did," the sheep said.

Nancy felt overwhelmed by the moment, the heaviness of it. "The peccary said water is near. Let's drink, find some food and rest for the night. Maybe tomorrow will bring us more guidance."

They found the watering hole easily, a small victory after a hard day of losses.

Exhausted, each animal lapped up the water even though it had a toxic tinge. Nancy drank the most. As she did, she heard a noise, a human noise, but it wasn't the noise of the crop duster. It was the noise of a jeep. Once again she saw the cow, her pain relieved now. Behind her a little calf on wobbly legs clung to her mother's tail.

The noise of the automobile was getting louder. The group of elephants, all females except the bull she'd first seen as a grey calf, was wary of the approaching sound. The elephants stood near a river, a river they couldn't cross. To the north was a large butte that they couldn't climb. To the east was a dense cluster of fever trees they had chewed on earlier that day. To the south was the road. And on that road was the human car, getting closer and closer...

"Nancy, I don't feel good," said Joe.

"Neither do we," said the horses.

"Me too," squeaked the monkey.

"The water is no good," said Nancy. "It's human water. It's no good. Why wouldn't the peccary tell us this?"

The animals were sick all that evening and into the night. Weak, vomiting, sleepless. When the zebra finally found sleep, the monkey woke her up with his sickness. And then the zebra woke up the baboon with hers and then the baboon woke Joe with his. Round and round.

During those times when they believed Nancy was too sick to hear them, the collective ventured towards mutiny.

"She's led us nowhere."

"We were better off with the humans. The tiger was right." This caused to group to look for him, lurking in the shadows. He was out there somewhere.

"Those animals, they were mostly small. We can catch up with them tomorrow."

"What if the plane returns?"

"And now she gets us sick."

"She will soon get us killed."

"We'll leave her tomorrow."

Joe heard all of this. He didn't speak up. He didn't know what to do. He understood their complaints. He wouldn't leave Nancy, but he understood why they wanted to. His stomach was better able to deal with toxicity than the others' and he threw up only once. Otherwise, he rested near Nancy. As the animals continued to complain about her, he saw that she was awake and listening.

Those beautiful brown eyes of hers, looking sad and despondent, hid themselves under the heavy lid, not wanting to see Joe, not wanting to see anything.

But it did see something. It saw the rest of her story. Her father's story. Her father was the grey calf who'd grown up, who was trapped by the humans who'd approached with their car. It was also her mother's story; her mother's fate was intertwined with that of the bull elephant who gave Nancy life.

That bull—Nancy's father—was poached for his ivory, those powerful tusks he had used to spar and tear and protect. He'd helped the cow elephants and the calves find safety behind the fever trees. But the humans arrived before he himself could hide. They shone the lights of their jeeps and he was exposed. A quick shot from a rifle maimed him and made him angry. The jeep had come to a stop. Three humans ran out, guns aimed at his grey body. They shot him again. The bullet entered his sternum, blowing him back, but he found a way to get his momentum going forward. Another shot. He was blown back again. And again he found the strength to inch forward. Two more shots and he couldn't move anymore. He was done.

Nancy, the young calf, was witness to it all. She watched from behind the lush fever trees as the humans sharpened knives and cut into her father's skin, even as he still drew breath. They ignored his blood. They ignored his grunts. They ignored everything but the dull white of ivory.

After they'd taken what they were after, the humans climbed back into the jeep and rumbled, then faded, into the night. Nancy was just a yearling; she'd had no idea it was possible to feel such sadness, sadness that slowed her toward paralysis.

After a time, the herd stepped out from the shadows. They circled Nancy's father, heads hung low, ears pulled back. When it was finally her mother's turn to say goodbye, Nancy let go of her tail and watched her mother slowly circle the carcass. She circled again and again and finally she collapsed to her knees. There, her sadness overtook her and she collapsed from her knees toward her side. And then, incredibly, Nancy watched as her mother shut her eyes and died.

The laughing hyenas were waiting. A lion roared, jarring Nancy, making her remember that threats were everywhere. Then it was her turn. To circle her dead mother and murdered father. She felt her mother's sadness. She nuzzled that big body, which was still warm. Her mother had so much more to teach. As did her father. How was Nancy going to learn? Should she join them? She looked at the holes in her father's body, which already reeked of decay, and she looked at her mother, stuck forever to the ground, and she made a pact with herself to remember this moment for the rest of her life, as though it were as much a part of her as her blood and bones. But she didn't. She'd forgotten. And now Nancy realized that being aware meant more than trying to understand the present, or planning for the future. It meant knowing the past, and all the pain, or joy, that memories brought.

Bear

The bear watched the black bear descend to the battlefield below. When he reached the bottom of the cliff, he looked back up and waved the bear down. When the bear ignored the request, the black bear turned and charged toward the front lines. The bear watched him disappear into the fray.

The bear could just make out the city near the horizon when an explosion lit up the dark with brilliant colors. The bear had often seen the sky put on a show of lights deep inside night's darkness. But he had never seen such vivid lights erupt from just one small area. This wasn't the sky speaking. This was something the humans had created. It was beautiful, the bear thought, but sad, for he knew this beauty came at a cost.

The bear felt oddly calm as he watched the mural of warfare spread before him. For the time being he was satisfied just to watch, to see human and animal attack each other. He didn't ask himself how this started. He knew, somehow, that the time was right, that perhaps this war had been in the works for years, decades, eons.

He wondered what the humans were thinking. Had they seen this coming? Were they prepared? They seemed to be. Or maybe they were always prepared to fight. There were maybe a thousand of them, all armed, slaughtering whatever animals they could shoot down or slice up.

As he looked down at the animals, fighting back, fighting strong, the bear had a guess as to why the battle below him was fought with so much vigor by the mammals. Their anger toward humans was tangible. It was everywhere. If the awareness had never occurred, would the anger be any less apparent? He feared the simple answer was no, it wouldn't be apparent at all.

He would have loved to have seen the look on the humans' faces when the initial attack began. Those funny creatures, with their delicate heads, their childlike vulnerability, being mauled by four-legged attackers. What did a human think when an otter went after him in the shallows of the river? Did he care? But what did he think when a thousand otters attacked?

And what did humans think when bears attacked? The bear assumed the humans would fear him more than the other animals; he was so much larger, quicker, and smarter, with teeth and claws that could make rag dolls of the humans' precarious skin and weak bones. Who would fear a deer? But his dangerousness also made him the most obvious target, and the bear knew the damage those guns could do.

Below his perch he watched as a young buck, recently antlered, came out from nowhere to gore an unsuspecting young human, who was reloading his gun. The bear could almost taste the human's blood as it sprayed high into the air. The young human fell to the dirt, coiling into a pose of certain death. The bear swelled with pride as he watched these lesser animals do everything they had to do. They had it so much harder than the bear, than the humans, but they fought with such stoic concentration. Always looking up, always staring into the sun, always looking behind and underneath and through. They had the most to fight for. Every fight for them was life or death—usually death.

I need to help them, the bear thought. But he didn't want to join. He didn't know why. The others had rushed into battle without questioning their speed. Even the other bears. They were still coming from the forest, from the hills, running, charging, dashing forward. But here he was, sitting, watching. It wasn't as though he didn't want the animals to win. But what did he want for himself?

He'd just killed a human for the first time in his life. It hadn't really given him any sense of satisfaction. Perhaps only those animals who'd been harmed by humans wanted to harm them back now.

A black cloud circled above him. He looked closer: not a cloud after all but a dense flock of nighttime flyers. These dark creatures swooped down closer to him than they should have. He tried to swat them away, but they were too fast.

Bats, he thought.

"We need you," he heard the bats say, a hissing chorus. "Don't just sit there. This is our chance. The time is now."

"I don't know."

"There is nothing to know. This is the time to do."

"I'm thinking."

"This isn't the time to think. We'll have all the time in the world after the war is over."

"Go and attack and leave me be."

The bats soared down to the battlefield, but another flying creature took their place. The hawk circled above and then landed on the grassy expanse, ten feet from where the bear sat watching the battle below.

"What do you want?" the bear said.

The hawk hopped about on its thin legs, somewhere between graceful and awkward. He delivered a loud caw.

"Stop that," growled the bear. But the bird didn't seem to understand—maybe he couldn't communicate the way the mammals could. The hawk hopped nearer, into swatting distance. His eyes, void of anything other than blackness, were unwavering. He was nearly looking through the bear.

When the shots went off below, flashes of the battlefield became clear. Even from his vantage point far above the warfare, it was evident that the animals were losing many of their own.

The problem, the bear realized, is the guns were keeping the animals at too great a distance. "Once we get to the humans, they have no chance. They need to change strategy." The bear considered his statement. "We need to change strategy," he corrected himself.

The hawk dipped her head, turned her neck, flapped her wings. Then she flew off.

She was too fast and it was too dark for the bear to follow her flight. It occurred to him: The birds weren't on either side. They were watching. They weren't choosing.

The bear closed his eyes. The birds didn't need to choose, but he did. It was foolish to sit here, alone, watching the carnage. It was cowardly, and he wasn't a coward, even though he didn't feel the same impulse to fight as the other animals seemed to feel. He wondered why. Then he realized that he could spend the rest of his life wondering. He would never leave the ledge.

"They might need me," he told no one but the air. He thought again of his mother, feeding him the salmon she'd caught. She'd want him to help, especially if some of those fighting below couldn't help themselves. He should have saved the fawn, he knew. He should have told her to run and hide and protect herself.

He climbed down the rocky ledge, nearly slipping a few times before jumping the final gap to the ground and landing with a resounding thud. He reared up on his haunches and roared his loudest roar. It was time.

The first thing he wanted to do was round up the wolves and any other bears he could find. Instead of charging to the front lines he went to the back, where the wounded were being tended. Two beavers were attempting to mend the bullet hole in a badger's shoulder. Mice were picking out bloody debris trapped in the matted fur of a disabled moose. The bear approached the beavers first.

"Who's in charge of this attack?"

The beavers drew away from the bear. Even in the heat of battle old habits lingered.

"I'm not here to harm you," the bear reassured them.

"No one is," one of them said. "Except the humans." The beavers resumed their work on the badger. The bear moved in closer; the badger was clearly in pain but doing his prideful best not to show it. "You doing okay, friend?"

"As best as can be expected." The badger let out a guttural wail. The bear guessed he would be dead in minutes.

Being near all these animals was hard for the bear. He preferred to be alone. But he knew his mother would have preferred to eat the salmon for herself and yet she fed him. These were not times of solitude.

"We need to organize. Mice. Come here, please."

The mice scurried to the base of the bear's enormous frame.

"You live with the humans more than most. You sneak around them. You know them better than any of us."

The mice talked in unison. The bear couldn't understand. He let out a polite roar. The mice quieted, several disappearing under his fur, hiding. Then one spoke for all.

"Yes. We do. They seldom know we're there. We've been watching them forever."

"What do you know?"

"They hate us. They leave food everywhere and are surprised when we eat it. They hate rats even more. Humans are one hundred times our size but we instill fear in them."

"Why would someone fear you and the rats?"

"We don't know, but we use it to our advantage. Oh, and this particular clan of humans loves to shoot those guns. They all have them."

"I can see that," the bear said. The badger was breathing heavily, his whine now a death rattle. "We need to disarm them and then attack with the wolves, bears, badgers. What we can't do is sneak up on them. But you can. You must take them by surprise, bite their ankles and toes, crawl up their legs. If they really are afraid of you, they will be busy fending you off, and then we can charge."

"We can do that," said the mouse.

"Gather every small rodent and tell them the plan. I will tell the top predators."

The mouse and his cohorts scattered over the battlefield, whispering the new strategy.

The bear looked over at the badger, who looked back with unseeing eyes, then coughed and died. The bear put his huge paw on the badger's face and whispered to him. Then he ran into the darkness behind the battle and told the others his plan; they repeated it, and soon the animals were organized. The bear tried to enjoy the feeling of camaraderie. He missed being alone, but there was something striking about working with other animals, rather than hunting and devouring them. Of the many new concepts flooding his mind, this was one of the most appealing but also discomfiting. He was hungry, and yet couldn't eat his soldiers.

The animals retreated to regroup. So did the humans. A cacophony of armaments and cries of death or temporary victory was replaced by an eerie silence. Only the birds overhead made a sound, pumping their wings against the wind coming in from the east. The earth seemed to take a deep breath. The bodies on the front lines remained where they had fallen, ugly lumps of stiffening carbon. Soon, they'd be fodder for the flies—and perhaps for some of the soldiers, animals who wouldn't eat their fellow compatriots alive, but would devour a fresh corpse.

In the distance, the bear could see lights from the cigarettes of the humans, tiny orange bursts.

"I don't see why we can't just attack them like we do our prey," said the wolf-pack leader, a dignified animal with a silver coat that resembled the moon.

"Not even you, friend, can outwit a gun," the bear offered.

"And you think mice and rats can?"

"I do. Humans don't know what to make of us. They admire us for our beauty and power. They fear us because we are stronger. That fear is rational. Their fear of rodents is not rational. We will use this weakness. The rodents will sneak up on the humans as they aim those guns, climb up their legs."

"It seems too simple a plan," the wolf said.

"Do you have another? Because as I watched from atop the cliff, I saw the humans massacreing us."

The wolf pack was wary of the bear. The bear knew this, and while he wasn't afraid of them individually, he knew they demanded respect as a unit. Four of the wolves rose up and began circling the bear.

"We must not fight among ourselves," the beavers pleaded. "We need all of you, the bears and the wolves, if we are going to win this."

The old silver-haired wolf bared his teeth and then stopped.

"Yes. You're right." He shot a purposeful glare at the four who were circling, and they fell back behind him.

"If this doesn't work, we can pull back and try something else," the bear offered.

"We need to do it now, then," the wolf said. "If we wait too long, day will break and then the humans will have the advantage. They have other weapons. Flying machines. Poisons. We are evenly matched in the night. The day belongs to them."

The bear nodded.

He beckoned for the mice and rats. Scores and scores came to him, a speckled blanket of fur and tails.

"You know what to do, friends?"

An affirmative murmur.

"Get to it then. They will shoot some of you. Many of you will live. Be brave, be quick, be relentless. Tap into their fear of you. Tap into it and don't let go. Our friends in the sky, the bats, will be watching as we creep slowly toward the front lines. When we hear the signal that the rodents have attacked, the guns will drop. The wolves and the moose and the elk will attack with the full force of nature."

The rodents were off. The bear watched the orange bursts. As the stealthy rodents neared the humans, the predators and larger prey waited patiently. In this lull in the battle they could hear the sobbing and lowing of the wounded, the occasional blast of a gun, a muffled cry.

Then, just as they got used to this quiet, the air was broken by noise. The bear and the rest of the infantry heard the human screams. From ahead and above, the bats shrieked ferociously.

"Now!" the bear yelled.

The rodents were right. The humans hated them. Even the strongest of the humans, the ones with the deepest voices and the thickest beards, screamed as the vermin attacked. They dropped their guns, their coats and trousers. The ground moved with grey uneasiness; the vermin were living grass and wind. The bear ran toward his new prey, and, running, he met up with the black bear. The bear had assumed the worst when he couldn't find the black bear's scent nor see his scarred visage.

"Where have you been?"

"Fighting. I thought you'd stay on that bluff forever."

"I might have. But here I am."

"This was your plan?"

"It was. Sometimes to watch and think is more valuable than to act."

"And what did you see up there?"

"Everything."

"Let's go."

The two bears ran ahead, looking to wound.

As the bear charged, time slowed. He could feel the core of the earth reverberate up to his chest each time his paw struck the sod. Some new synaptic connection linked him with every animal that wanted victory and feared defeat. He had singular focus. Find the humans, avoid the bullets, and kill. Not for his own protection. He didn't need protection from humans. But for the mice, the rats, the beavers, the lesser animals who'd fed him and his brethren for so long. For the dead fawn.

As he charged, as he growled and postured, new words flooded his mind. He knew what corporeal meant, and he could feel his body in a way he never had before. He was aware of his actions, aware of why he stretched and roared and ran. He understood his purpose. He understood cause and effect. He understood power. He understood that humans knew more of power than any other species, that this knowledge alone made them special. He understood that he had power, that he'd had it all along; he could feel it with each stride. He had seen his own power in the face of the hare, the humans, the beavers, the mice, but he hadn't been able to harness it like the humans.

He ran toward his destiny. As he did, he thought of his mother's den, of his brother, of the new life awaiting him if he survived.

The lines of combat met. A wolf tore into a human, ripping apart the jugular. Three ferrets gnawed at another human's midsection.

Not all the humans had dropped their arms, despite the success of the rodent assault. A human got off a shot and an elk fell on his hindlegs. He buckled. He died.

The black bear killed four humans in a matter of seconds. His assault was magnificent, like an empire taking its first crushing steps.

The bear wished his brother were here with him, fighting at his side. Together, he and his brother, they would have conquered everything.

The battle waged on. The bear's plan was working. The predators were killing. The humans, when disarmed, were nothing but rotten berries to be picked off a vine and chewed up.

Dawn. The bear ebbed back, away from the battle. He was exhausted. His bones ached and he needed to rest, so he climbed up into the rocks where he'd spent the previous night. Again, he watched. The battle's ferocity had dimmed, and the bear could see the results: bodies of every species bleeding from punctures and wounds, limbs severed; all the things, deserved and cruel, that happen in a battle. He stayed crouched in his slice of safety. A confused human, wounded by rat bites, by a wolf's swat, by hunger and exhaustion, crawled toward him, so dazed he didn't know he was talking to a bear.

"Yesterday I was on my way to work." The human was dark haired, the heaviness of everything pulling down the skin below his listless blue eyes, which were puffy with bruises. His clothes had been ripped and were shredded at the hems. The man couldn't catch his breath.

The bear thought of those salmon. He couldn't stop his heart from feeling the man's pain.

"It's been a rough few hours," the man said.

"Tell me why."

The man looked at him. Now he realized he was talking to a bear. The man laughed, but it wasn't a mocking laugh, nor was it joyful. It was scared and incredulous. Everything that had happened over these last hours—none of it made sense. This made no more or less sense.

"I don't understand what's going on, but I think you're going to win."

"Why?"

"Because we don't understand what we're fighting. We don't have the right weapons. We made our weapons to fight each other. No one ever told us we were going to do battle with you."

The bear thought this over. "Did you have a mother?"

"Of course."

"Did you have a brother?"

"No. I have three sisters."

The bear looked at him closely. The human was so frail, so white, so vulnerable—and so hurt. His body was riddled with bites, his mind by guilt.

"I know guilt now, too," the bear said.

"I don't know what that means."

"I killed humans the way you kill us. It felt good, but then it felt bad."

The man started to shed tears. "How can I hear this bear, this beast? Please, kill me. End it."

"No."

"Why?"

"I need to understand more. Come."

The bear picked up the wounded human and carried him up the steep incline. He dropped him upon his earlier perch, and the two of them watched the battle. The human started coughing violently.

"You need care," the bear said. He picked up the human again and brought him to the den. The human was weak, and his frailty was beginning to annoy the bear.

"Please kill me," he repeated. "I have nothing to go back to."

The bear shut him up with a growl.

Once inside, the man collapsed into a deep sleep. The bear went back outside and picked at some insects from inside a log. After he ate his fill, he cupped his paws and took some for the human.

The human made noises as he slept. Was he remembering something? Finally, the human stirred, stretched, then sat up.

"Where am I?"

"The place where I rest. Here. I brought you food." He extended his paws to the human.

The human, seeing the insects, shook his head. "Thank you. But we don't eat that."

The bear shrugged. "I have things I need to ask you."

"And then you'll kill me?"

"Why do you keep talking about death?"

"Do you not know what's going on?"

"Tell me."

"Animals are fighting us everywhere. Africa, Asia, Europe. Our world is over."

"Your world?"

"As we knew it."

"What did you like best about your world?"

The man pondered this. "What do you mean?"

"What is your favorite part of being human?"

"Sex," the man said, and then laughed without conviction.

"Sex? To have offspring?"

"No, to have fun. We have fun when we mate. It's what makes our world go around."

"I think you're wrong. I think the best part of being human is how well you adapt. And so swiftly. How you conquer. You are able to pull together different thoughts, plans, and actions in a way the rest of us can't."

"Until now."

"Until now."

"And what about you?" the man asked.

"What about me?"

"What was it like before? Do you remember?"

The bear laughed. "Of course. I can only speak for myself, but I was aware of everything I needed to be aware of. There wasn't as much going on in my mind as now. I didn't have all these words, but I had the same feelings. And maybe I did have thoughts. They were just different. That is all. It would be like me asking you if you knew how to chew because your teeth aren't as sharp as mine."

"I see," said the human.

"Do you?"

"No," the human said. "Not really."

"Tell me more about being human. Tell me about your mother," the bear said. For a while the man remained silent. He looked overwhelmed and defeated. The bear didn't press him. He picked at the insects.

"Why would you be interested in my mother?"

"I don't know. I just can't stop thinking about my own mother. About that feeling I felt when I was next to her."

"How do you eat those?"

The bear looked down at the insect and shrugged. Then he dropped one into his mouth. The man smiled.

"I loved my mother. I was raised on a farm. We grew corn. Farm living is tough and outdated. But she made it fun. She woke us up early with breakfast, she was always laughing, helping us enjoy our lives. She was religious. She read to us from the Bible every morning. Then we'd do chores. There were four of us, so the workload wasn't too bad."

"Four offspring? Did your mother watch you closely?"

"I suppose. But not really. We each had a job to do, and we knew how to do it. Then we went to school, came home, did our homework, and were free to play the rest of the day away. Then, before we went to sleep, Mom would come to each of us separately, sit with us, talk to us one-on-one, so that we always felt special."

"What would she say?"

"Oh, sometimes she'd tell us something funny Dad did, or maybe ask us how school went. My favorite was when she'd tell me about the day I was born. I came two weeks early. She was riding in an elevator when it got stuck between floors. No one came to help, she panicked, and soon she went into labor. A stranger happened to be in there with her. The poor man was an accountant. But he delivered me and from then on he was invited to every Thanksgiving and every Christmas." The human smiled.

"You humans need help delivering your young?"

"Yes."

"And this stranger just helped out, even though he didn't have to?"

"It was the right thing to do."

"I don't understand humans."

"I don't either."

The bear yawned. His head ached from all these thoughts. "I think I have learned enough for now. I would invite you to stay here with me, but that isn't wise, I fear."

"No."

"Would you like me to take you back?"

"I can walk. I could use the fresh air."

"What are you going to do?"

"I'm going to go home, if I still have a home. I want to talk to my mother."

"She's still alive?"

"She was two days ago."

"Does she live with you?"

"No. She still lives where I grew up. Many, many miles from here."

The bear thought about this. "Say hello from me."

The human laughed. So did the bear.

"And I was wrong before," the human said. "The best part of being human isn't sex. It's love. That's what separates us from you. We can love with the same intensity that you hunt."

The bear nodded. "How would you define this love?"

"I can't. It's just something you feel for another human."

The bear thought about his own family. "I loved my mother too, I think. But I didn't realize it until now. At least, I didn't realize that it was love."

"Is she alive?"

"I don't know."

The human said nothing. The two sat there for a long time in the safety of silence.

"What are you going do?" the human finally asked. "Go back and fight?"

"No," the bear said. The bear knew he needed to learn more. He wasn't ready to fight just yet.

The two creatures looked at each other. The bear, without understanding why, stood and hugged the human, gently, trying to express something, perhaps kindness, or sympathy, without hurting the fragile creature. The human, though startled at first, hugged the bear back. He began to cry.

The two creatures parted. The human walked into the sunlight, grabbed a branch from the forest floor, and used it to steady his gait. The bear closed his eyes. This time, when all the thoughts deluged his mind, he'd sort them out. A plan was forming amid all the dreams and reflections.

He wasn't so sure that the human was right. Love was very important. But so was hope, and kindness, and empathy. And there was something else, too. He didn't have a word for it. But it was that thing that humans used to survive, to thrive, to succeed. Because that's what they did. All of them. Everywhere.

"Creation." The word just came to him. Creation.

Dog

They'll be back, Clio had told him. It was all he could think about. Jessie had boarded up the windows, including the one in the room where Cooper had found Clio hiding. But the cat slipped back into a dark corner whenever Jessie was present. Why was she hiding? Clio was smarter than he was, he knew that even before the awareness, and he figured she must have had a reason to keep herself out of sight.

The door at the top of the stairs felt secure. The walls seemed unbreakable. But none of those obstacles would stop the animals. Nothing would prevent them from finding a way in, from turning on him, the treasonous dog, and from tearing into Jessie's summer skin, already bronzed and tender from days in the park and at the beach.

He let the image of Jessie's dead corpse, her flesh stuck to the teeth of his fellow mammals, ebb into the recesses of his new mind. Now he wondered: Did the other animals know what he had done? There were so many thoughts in the air now and inside him. It was too confusing; he didn't like confusion. He remembered what it was like to ponder a bone, that wonderful white piece of calm.

He forced himself to think of something else, of anything other than the barriers that had to come down, the fate that seemed preordained by the rats and the raccoons.

Carol was up again, walking about. Her movements were frenetic; she was like a wounded animal, like prey. Jessie was pacing, pensive now, daydreaming away the reality of war. Her eyes squinted though there was no sun, and the creases next to them aged her. Her pacing had a soporific effect on Cooper, like a pendulum. Happily, his mind wandered. He thought of strange things. His food bowl. His collection of plastic toys.

The feeling of the leash on his neck. Remembrances bound by fondness, simple pleasures.

"We're trapped in here," Jessie said, her worried tone piercing his thoughts.

Cooper lifted his head.

"What do you mean?"

"Trapped. Confined. By the floor, and by the planks over the windows. It's like we're just sitting here waiting for them to come back."

Had Jessie read his thoughts? Were they floating around in the air, free for anyone to grab and understand?

"We can't leave, Jessie," he said.

"I know. They might be up there. They might be waiting. I don't know. I don't know what the right thing is."

Her pacing quickened. She raced around the perimeter of the room. Carol ignored her, muttering to herself.

"Jessie," Cooper said. "Please."

"I just keep thinking this has to be a dream. I keep thinking that Peter will turn up any moment, tell me he loves me again, we'll all be together back it in the apartment. Having sex again."

"Jessie!" Carol said. So she wasn't as remote as Cooper had thought.

"What?" Jessie asked. "What, mother?"

Carol didn't answer.

"It's not a dream," Cooper said quietly. "It's not even a nightmare. It's real."

Jessie nodded and then sat down, her back against the wall. Stillness eased itself into the room. Their breathing was uniform. They made no sudden movements. The threats that loomed over them seemed easier to comprehend, easier to endure, when perfecting an almost meditative silence.

Cooper played along. He was watchful, but he acted indifferent. Again, his mind wandered. This constant drifting had to be part of having awareness. It roamed from topic to topic, like it was tracing debris on a sidewalk late at night, as when Jessie and Peter would take him down Houston, where the vomit and the litter warranted his pressing attention.

What did he want? What did he want?

The answers that came to him would have been a fool's choice mere hours ago. He wanted to know why humans smoked cigarettes. He wanted to understand why humans didn't mind thunder. He wanted to look into the eyes of the man who had ripped him from his mother's teat, and to understand the exact hold the mailman had over him. He wanted to drink coffee, to enjoy food without devouring it, to grasp Christmas, open a present. He wanted to rescue those who couldn't rescue themselves. He wanted to be like Jessie.

But then he didn't. Maybe he just wanted to understand what it meant to be a dog in her world, to understand his old life in the new context of awareness. Every dog has its day. Let a sleeping dog lie. The dog days of summer. Humans thought they knew the connection between dog and man. Pet. Cooper couldn't figure the word out, the concept. To be both revered and imprisoned.

And he couldn't understand the endless streams of this new mind, calm eddies, spinning rapids, tumbling waterfalls. He would learn to swim through it all with time. If only he had enough of it.

Carol was staring at him. Her eyes had lost some of their clarity.

"What?" he asked. "What?"

She shook her head and looked away. What had she been thinking? He'd saved her life. Did she want him dead? Did she blame him for this morning's events?

"The radio," she said.

"The radio?" Jessie repeated.

"You should have brought a radio with you. Or a phone. Or something we could use to hear what's going on."

"For goodness' sake, Mom, we didn't have time to think. Cooper dragged you down here and saved your life. We were being attacked."

"We need a radio," Carol said. Then she muttered a few words to herself and turned away.

"Actually, she's right," Jessie admitted. "We do need to know what's going on outside."

"Where is it?" Cooper asked.

"Mom's is in the kitchen cabinet."

Cooper cocked his ears, listening for movements on the floorboards above. "I don't hear anything. Maybe it's safe. I can get it."

"No, let me," Jessie said.

"No," Cooper said firmly.

They stopped talking, both attuned to any noises upstairs. Carol was engaged in a quiet conversation that began and ended in her dreams. "Shh!" Jessie said. Carol stopped muttering for a moment.

"I don't hear anything," Cooper said. "Come with me to the top of the stairs. Open the lock, I'll run out and grab it."

"How will you do that?" Carol asked, her voice cracking. "How will you do that without hands? Without being human? Answer me that."

The other two ignored her. They went to the top of the stairs, put their ears next to the door. Nothing.

"Okay," Cooper said. "Now."

Jessie turned the lock and opened the door just enough for Cooper to squeeze through.

Cooper looked around. Someone or more than someone had been here. Furniture was strewn about, dishes lay smashed on the floor. Odd they hadn't heard anything. Or maybe this mess was the result of the earlier fight. Cooper hadn't had time to map out the environment before they dashed downstairs.

The bodies of the animals were still there. Still dead, but fresh. Cooper drooled. Some primal instinct taunted him.

He shook his head and ran to the kitchen, to the radio on the counter. More bodies. Dead.

But perched on the other counter opposite were four very alive bats.

The bats looked at Cooper. Cooper looked at the bats.

For a moment, no one spoke. Then one of the bats asked, "Where did you come from?"

Cooper's mind raced. The bats were small but lethal. Sharp-toothed. Quick. Smart. Rats with wings. He couldn't take them all.

"Outside. I live nearby. I want this." He used his eyes to point to the radio.

"Why?" another bat asked.

"It's a form of communication. Humans talk to each other through it. We can learn."

Another of the bats was eyeing him suspiciously. "Why are you alone? No one's alone."

"Not alone," Cooper said. "With a cat. And some others."

"Dogs?"

"What?"

"Dogs have been a problem. Many of them haven't joined the revolution. Some are fighting alongside their humans."

Cooper tried not to look like a dog who had killed his kind. He wondered if blood had crusted on his lips. But no, Jessie would have cleaned that off for him. Jessie.

The bats glared at him. Eight angry, beady eyes focused on his. "Where are yours?"

"My what?"

"Your humans?"

"I don't know," he said. Weak, he thought. He didn't like lying. To anyone. It wasn't his nature.

"Who killed our comrades?" another bat asked.

"I don't know," Cooper lied again. "But it must have been humans. See how they've been shot. Humans shoot."

They can sense my fear, Cooper thought. Don't show fear. But his fear stank.

The largest of the bats suddenly smiled, a slash of crooked teeth. "It's okay," he said. His voice was strangely soothing. "You don't have to be afraid of us. I bet those humans were very good to you. They probably saved your life. Brought you in. Loved you. Of course you helped them. You're a good dog. You've been loyal and you're kind. But don't you feel it? Can't you hear it?"

Cooper cocked an ear.

"The revolution is calling you, dog. It's calling all of us. We all feel it. Stop thinking about your humans. Listen to the call."

Cooper listened. And he heard something. Something he hadn't heard until now. Something inside him connecting with this outside sound, with billions of other mammals. A golden field of connection. Rage trickled into his mind, the fury of his kind.

"I do feel it," he said, hesitating.

"I know you can feel it," the bat said. "We all do. All of us." He paused. "Now tell us where the humans are."

Thoughts, emotions, feelings welled inside Cooper. He started to growl, he imagined his teeth sinking into a human, wreaking vengeance. He felt thousands of mouths devouring humans. He felt anger, he felt blood.

Then the human in his mind, the one whose flesh he was devouring, looked up. Jessie. He was sinking his teeth into

Jessie. He would not hurt Jessie. His anger dissipated, drifted away...He thought about Jessie...the silence...the bats weren't used to this silence.

"Where are the humans?" another bat snapped.

"There are no humans here," Cooper said. "I have to go back to the cat." He grabbed the radio with his mouth.

"No," said the large bat. But Cooper's sharpness had returned, and it took just a few seconds to sprint back to the basement door, which Jessie was still holding open. She slammed it shut. A split second later they heard the crash of bats flying into wood. The animals were too small to do serious damage.

"We'll come back," they shrieked. "We know where you are. We know what you're doing."

Cooper and Jessie ran down the stairs. Carol looked up at them blankly, but then saw the radio and ran toward it, grabbing it from Cooper's mouth and putting it on top of an old cabinet. She turned it on. "Shh," Jessie said, flipping through stations. Most of them were out, but finally they found one.

"...Nothing is clear," the announcer said. "But the biggest battles are taking place in the states along the East Coast and the Great Lakes. In the South, many of the larger cities have fallen. In the West, San Francisco and Seattle have been able to hold out..." Static. Fadeout.

"No!" Carol pounded on the radio. It came back to life. "For now the best advice is to stay put. But if you can't, there are fortified shelters springing up all over the country. Here in New York, you can find a list at..."

Static. Carol hit the radio again. "Do not attempt to get to the shelters yourself. Armored buses and tanks are crisscrossing the state. Wait until you see one. Flag it down..."

Static. "It's the batteries," Carol said. "They're dead. I don't use them. Why didn't you bring the cord?"

"I didn't see one," Cooper said.

She turned off the radio. "There are batteries down here. Somewhere. I'll find them."

She didn't get more than a few feet before they heard an odd noise from the boiler room.

"What was that?" Jessie asked.

"You go," Carol said to Cooper. He looked at her—for a moment, he saw trust in her eyes. Or maybe she just didn't care what happened to him.

He approached the room cautiously. Did animals get inside? How? There were no windows. Perhaps the walls had given way? The foundation had rotted in several places.

Cooper entered. He looked. He sniffed. The smell of the oil was unpleasant, even though the boiler had been turned off for months. But now he went a little further into the room. And smelled blood. Around the corner, behind the boiler.

He approached quietly. And then he saw. Two humans, a man and a woman. The woman was badly wounded. Both humans were asleep. The man's foot had knocked over an old can of oil, which was leaking onto the floor.

Cooper recognized them.

The man, Larry, was a gardener—he was tall, scrawny, with wisps of unkempt hair. He helped Carol plant flowers. Sometimes he threw a tennis ball for Cooper to chase. The woman was his girlfriend. Mary Lee, Cooper thought, although until now he hadn't known he knew her name. He must have heard it, stored it somewhere. Or perhaps it was another of these thoughts that seemed to float into the air, like scents ready to be picked up, followed.

He ran back to Jessie. "Come," he said. As she entered the room the couple woke up.

"Oh, my God." Jessie knelt down to help. Cooper stayed in the background. "I guess we fell asleep," Larry said. He brushed the hair out of Mary Lee's face, stood up and stretched his arms, yawning loudly. Then he spotted Cooper.

"Jesus. What is that *goddamn thing* doing here?" he asked.

Cooper retreated while Larry and Jessie carried Mary Lee into the other room and lay her on a blanket. Carol wandered over. "Something got her bad," she said before returning to her corner.

"*Squirrels*," Larry said. He spat the word. "We were attacked by *squirrels*."

Mary Lee moaned. Her face was bleeding. Jessie found a roll of paper towels, wet them, and tried cleaning her wounds.

"Get that dog out of here," Larry said. "He hasn't turned yet? He will."

"He saved our lives," Jessie said. Her firm voice kept Larry quiet for a moment. Cooper remained in the background.

"I found batteries," Carol said. But when she put them in the radio, nothing happened. "Dead," she said. "Like Sally. Like everything." She sat on the floor and put her hands over her head.

"Mary Lee needs help," Larry said. He pressed her body against his chest. "We can't stay here anyway. They'll get us."

"Where are we going to go?" Jessie asked. "The radio said..."

"Screw the radio. What time is it?"

"Three o'clock,"

"Christ," Larry said. "We got attacked. We ran in here. Fell asleep."

He looked at Cooper. "We've got to leave."

"You won't get far," Cooper said. "We're safe here."

"Until you decide to kill us. You and your friends."

Jessie shook her head. "There are animals everywhere. We can stay here until we figure out something better to do."

"There isn't anything better to do than leave." Larry examined Mary Lee's face. She was conscious, but wordless.

Then, another immense boom, from somewhere above. Things seemed to be falling apart upstairs and through the house. Carol screamed. "What the hell was that?"

"It sounded like it came from the front of the house," Cooper said. "Like someone knocked out the front windows."

"Shhh." Jessie placed her finger to her mouth.

They don't need to hear you to know you're here, thought Cooper. But he said nothing.

Up above them, steps—some loud, some soft.

"They're coming." Carol began to sob. "Why is this happening to us?" she asked, again and again. She looked at Cooper. "This is your fault. You let this happen. You let them know we were here."

"Don't be crazy. Cooper saved your life. Why would he try to kill you now?"

"The old woman's right," Larry said.

"Cooper, do you know what they're doing?" Jessie asked.

"No."

The noise abated. Again, they all fell into silence, into their private fears. For a while, they were four people and a dog in a room, oblivious to each other and the world. Time passed, slowly, with nothing to do but wait, for what they didn't know.

Jessie was stroking Cooper's back. "Will you tell me something?" she asked.

"Sure."

"Was I good to you?"

"What kind of question is that?"

"I need to know. I need to know, if they knock down this door and kill me. Did you like your food? Did I walk you enough? Was I good to you?"

An album of images flipped through Cooper's mind. The dog park in snowfall. Jessie jingling the door with her keys. The treats he'd begged for, the stuffed toad he wanted to tug on, the stolen bits of food she fed to him under the table after he'd driven her crazy licking her calf.

"You were always good to me," he said. "Always."

Another loud crack came from above, this time followed by an odd sizzling sound. The lights surged bright as the north star and, just as suddenly, lost their luster. The electricity was out.

"Damn," Larry said.

The noises from upstairs ceased.

Cooper walked slowly up the stairs. He sniffed the crack between the floor and the bottom of the door.

"They're gone."

"How did they shut off the power?" Carol asked. "They couldn't," Jessie said. "The power probably went off everywhere."

Cooper looked down from the top of the stairs. What was there to see from this height? Anger, resolute anger. Entrapment. Fear.

He walked back down the stairs. The room was bathed in shadows.

He reached the bottom of the stairs, sat next to Jessie, and let her rub his chin.

"This is kind of what it felt like to be a dog, before. Things were always just a little dark. I see that now. Quiet and dark."

"We need to leave," Larry said. "Just get in your car and get the hell out of here."

"What do you think, Cooper?" Jessie found a large candle on one of the nearby shelves and lit it. The flickering light was not soothing.

"Who cares what *he* thinks? He's not coming," Larry said.

"This is the same dog you played fetch with."

"Jessie. No, he's not," Larry said.

"He goes wherever I go."

"I saw your car when we ran in here. It's in the driveway. We can make a run for it. Get in there, take off, get the hell out of Dodge."

"But the radio said not to," Jessie said.

"You won't get anywhere," Cooper added.

"It's not the animals outside who are going to kill us," Larry said, "It's that damn *mongrel* right there."

Cooper felt that primal rage surge again. Calm down, he instructed himself. Look at Jessie. He trotted over to her, put his face against her hand, forced her to pet him, to soothe him. How could he think these thoughts?

"You're maniacs if you think you can stay here." Larry was talking nonstop now. "You're insane. We're getting out of here. Where are the keys?"

Carol rifled through her purse, found the keys, handed them to Larry. He stuffed them in his jeans pocket.

"Don't do it," Jessie said.

"You coming?" Larry asked Carol.

"Yes."

"No," Jessie said firmly. "You're staying with us."

"You don't tell me what to do," Carol said. But she hesitated, muttering a few words.

"I'm not waiting for you to decide. The car's right in the driveway." Larry helped Mary Lee off the floor.

"Come on, baby. We're getting out of here." Mary Lee nodded. Cooper doubted she had any idea what was going on but she had always been willing to follow Larry.

Larry paused at the top of the steps. "Dog. Come here. Tell me if there's anyone in the house."

Cooper looked at Jessie, who nodded. He scaled the steps and sniffed the crack, cocking his ears. "Don't think so," he said. "But I could be wrong."

Larry had already made up his mind. With Mary Lee in his arms, he opened the basement door and slammed it behind him. They heard his heavy footsteps cross the living room floor; the front door opened, the old screen door screeching, whining, shutting. The car door slammed. The engine revved.

"We should have gone with him," Carol said. "I knew it."

The car shifted into gear.

And then, silence.

IV

ELEPHANT

FATHER NUZZLING. Mother caressing. The sense of love. Warmth, happiness. Nancy didn't want to waken. A moment of peace had enshrouded her, and she was afraid that any quick movement, any jarring experience, another barrage of bullets, might make her sacred image disappear like a mirage.

As orange streaks of early morning crisscrossed the east, Nancy spotted the tiger across the small lake. She nodded to him, he nodded back. She wondered how he had passed the night, but she soon dismissed her curiosity. Today was going to be different from yesterday, today was important. She flexed her leg, and it felt good. Her stomach was calm. The poison had left her system. Her head was clear.

She understood the other animals' feelings. She had shepherded them to nowhere in particular and nearly gotten them killed along the way.

"The monkey found fresh water!" Joe was running toward her—he and the monkey had gone out early on a scouting mission. "There's a small creek running into this lake, it's coming from a smaller pond not far away. The water is pure."

The other animals were all awake now.

"We don't care," the baboon said.

Slyly, the other animals had slid in behind the baboon, the way they had slid in behind Nancy a day and a half earlier.

"We want to go and catch up with the peccary and his team."

"We go where Nancy tells us to go," Joe said, trying to force an intimidating bleat into his words.

"You're free to leave," Nancy said. "I've told you I am no one's leader."

The sun had risen. The polluted water glimmered in the ascending light, giving the animals an odd aspect, making them strangely beautiful. Nancy watched their forms blur in this strange glow, these animals who had lived in the cages beside her and who had put their trust in her. She cared for them; she would miss them.

"You'll need water before you head out. Let's head up there, drink, and say goodbye. We've been working together for many years. If this is the last time I see you, I want it to be nice. I want nice memories."

The baboon turned and conferred with the others.

"We agree," he said, turning back. "Let us drink together one last time. As friends."

The animals walked up the path, Joe in the lead. Nancy followed Joe and the baboon followed her. Nancy felt a newfound calm. The stress of leadership, of constant care and worry, had been a burden.

After half an hour they found the small freshwater pond. Each animal lapped up the water with focused intent. Nancy remembered the watering hole of her dream, the different animals that had been present there; it was odd, but satisfying, to watch such a similar scene unfold in real life. Water had never tasted so good. She wanted to freeze this feeling.

"You need to stop them," Joe whispered to her. "We need them."

Nancy backed away from the water to a small cluster of shrubbery. Joe followed.

"We'll be fine. They need to leave."

"But what are we going to do?"

"Stay here. We have water. There's enough grass for you. And trees for me to pick at."

"But the war?"

"The fighting will come to us. Or we will get tired here and go after it. We don't need to make a decision now. We can take time to think, to collect ourselves. We've been lost for so long."

"We've only been lost because they stole us."

Nancy gazed at Joe. "You can go with them if you want."

Joe snorted and dipped his head between his front legs.

"Ridiculous." The word came out like water from a knotted hose, a reluctant spurt.

And then it happened. Nancy saw them first. Humans. They were hiding in the rows of tall cottonwoods.

The shots came quickly. An ambush.

"Run!" Nancy said this as soon as she saw the first human point a gun. The animals scattered. Water splashed. Hooves dotted the soft mud of the shore. Four new humans appeared in the brush. More shots. Errant shots. These humans weren't marksmen. They ducked after each shot, as if the animals might shoot back at them.

As Nancy ran, her anger festered. The humans ruin everything, she thought. Her anger fired through her synapses faster than any bullet.

Her parents were near. She could feel them.

The peccary was near, too. All at once, she felt the ghost of every circus animal, every caged creature, every tusk ripped from the flesh, moving through her.

"Joe," Nancy yelled.

"Meet me back behind that rock. I have a plan."

Joe sprinted behind the tall rock, which stood about one hundred yards east of the small lake. Nancy was out of breath when she reached the safety of the rock's shadow.

"What do we do?" asked Joe.

Nancy took a few deep breaths.

"We trap them. We don't kill them. We trap them."

"Why?"

"I need answers. I need to understand before I kill."

"Nancy..."

"Please. Get the others to join you. These humans aren't trainers. They're scared. I can smell their fear. They want us dead but they don't know how to kill properly. Sneak behind them. Trap them, Joe. Where's the monkey?"

But before Joe could trap the humans he had to get the animals to join the cause. Fortunately, they were eager to make amends on behalf of the baboon, who had been shot as he ran from the water. He had screamed, but his scream was lost to the fervor of the moment. Faking a limp and bathing in the attention, he then sprinted to where the sheep were hiding in the tall prairie grass.

Nancy had been correct. These humans were frightened. They had used their bullets. By the time a few of the more stealthy animals snuck up behind them, the humans had no choice but to wave their sunburned arms to the sky in surrender. One of the humans indicated to the others not to speak.

"Why?" Nancy asked. "Why not speak to us?"

The humans wouldn't respond. The sheep took the guns in their mouths and flung them into the lake. The monkey made a makeshift cord out of branches and tied up the humans, five in total, as best he could.

Nancy approached the baboon, leaned down, and waited for him to crawl up on top of her. She then walked determinedly towards the captives, the baboon sitting proudly on her back.

Nancy circled them, the way her mother had circled the dead body of her father.

The baboon, wincing in pain as if the wind affected his wound, glared down at them.

Two of the humans were adults. One started to weep. Nancy let her trunk feel the tears. The human recoiled at her touch.

"You won't speak, but you'll cry?" Nancy asked. "You know nothing of pain."

She wrapped her trunk around the youngest of the humans, pulling gently at her straw-like hair. This little human, with her straw head, was like all little humans who had cheered her in the tent, who had held the hands of the older humans or who had thrown peanuts, heckling her, too afraid to touch, or too bold, punching her when the older humans weren't looking.

The humans do everything for these little long-haired ones, Nancy thought. Even now the oldest humans, one male, one female, tensed up as her trunk wrapped around their progeny like an asp around a Nile reed.

Nancy put the little human down and turned her attention to the older ones. The one with the hair on his face, coarse and dark and flecked with grey, was the antithesis of the young female. He puffed his chest out, but his watering eyes gave him away.

I should step on him, Nancy thought. I should step on him and then watch the other humans cry, the way I cried when their kind killed my father.

The older female swatted away a fly. Nancy bent down and held her eyes a few inches from the female's lined face. This female human had burdens that the male did not. Nancy feared the look the female gave her, cold and steely. The male would attack, he would shoot his gun. But the female would plan. She would be patient.

Nancy went to one of the younger males, but she kept her stare on the old female. The young man tried to emulate his father by puffing out his chest.

"Cliff, stay quiet. Don't move. They can sense fear," the female said.

"How nice to have a mother to warn you," Nancy said to Joe and the others. "I wonder if they can smell this."

Nancy tightened her trunk and pushed the young male, who fell backward into the second young male, both falling to the ground.

The baboon laughed. Nancy remembered when the humans laughed at her as she pranced around the circus' stage.

The two humans tried to get up, but they only slipped in the mud.

This time the baboon and the horses laughed.

The two humans tried to regain their balance yet again. This time they succeeded, but Nancy pushed them until they were again writhing in the mud.

The baboon laughed again. Joe laughed. The giraffe smiled.

Then Nancy pushed over the biggest human. All the animals laughed. Nancy joined them. It felt good to laugh. It felt better to laugh at the humans.

"How many times had you laughed at us as we circled around the tents?" Nancy asked.

The animals took turns pushing the humans down. The laughter was contagious. It grew louder. And soon it was more than just laughter, it was a release, a reclamation of honor and power.

Finally, they used their laughter up. They were quiet. Nancy felt that this would be the time to kill the humans. That's what the peccary and his group would have done. She lowered herself so that the baboon could slide off of her prodigious back.

"You should do it," Nancy said as the baboon stepped off of her, still too wracked with pain to speak.

"I don't think I can," he said feebly, finally, and climbed back onto Nancy.

She stood up, her mind fogged. The blackbird cawed from above.

The animals looked skyward.

The blackbird cawed again, circled, then dove for the ground, fluttering as she approached, landing softly a few feet from Nancy. The bird cocked her head then bounced a few steps.

The bird's language wasn't clear. Her caws flew out like shrapnel, explosive, incomprehensible. Nancy guessed that the bird hadn't accepted the awareness—or wasn't offered it.

"You can join us, friend. We could use you, flying high, telling us who's coming," Nancy said. But the bird just cawed.

Nancy wondered. Mammals killed birds. Humans killed birds. Sometimes humans took care of birds. Mammals didn't. But humans killed birds in ways that mammals never would. There was no simple allegiance for the birds, so perhaps no choice had been made.

The blackbird stared at Nancy. She flapped her wings, but didn't take flight. A flock of monarch butterflies fluttered past. The blackbird opened her beak, snapped one up. She cawed, took a few small leaps, and flew away.

A dragonfly landed on Nancy's back. She flipped her tail up and knocked it away.

She thought of war, the sides one must take, the carnage, the loss, the wounds, the recklessness of it all. Who deserved to die? An insect? A butterfly? A bird? Her father, for nothing more than his ivory? The little human who was now clutching the loose, sweat-stained dress of her mother?

Nancy looked up at the bird, a black dot against the piercing blue. If only she could join her—she didn't know who deserved death and who life. And even so Nancy knew too much—too much of death, of loss, of war; she needed some relief.

"Just kill them and move on," the baboon said.

Nancy had an idea. "No," she said, firmly. "Not death. Something else."

The others didn't argue. But they didn't act either. They kept still. It was hot, they wanted to take a nap. While the baboon watched the humans, Joe and Nancy waded into the small lake.

"I keep thinking of why," Nancy said.

"Why?"

"Why."

She sprayed the water playfully at Joe, who wasn't as comfortable as Nancy in the muddy liquid.

"*Why.* Why do the humans do what they do?"

"Because they can?"

"I used to think that, before I was aware, before I could analyze my thoughts, or question them. But now I think it was something else. I think they control us, and even hurt us, to make themselves feel better about themselves."

Joe was watching silver guppies flit through the shallow water.

"That makes no sense."

"Nothing makes sense until it does. Humans captured us and made us dance to their tunes. They had a reason. Isn't there always a reason?"

Joe stared at her.

"Are you okay, Nancy?"

"Yes. I want to learn, Joe. What good is awareness if we don't use it? Let's do to them what they did to us. Let's teach them to amuse us, to do our bidding, lift our spirits."

Joe swiped his hoof at the nimble guppies. The splash wetted his face. "I don't get it."

"We've remembered. We've killed. It didn't make us feel any better. We got angry. We lost touch with our instincts. I forgot the one thing I promised myself I never would. We struggled. Why?"

"Because they took us?" Joe asked.

"Because they took everything that was ours and they made it theirs. Now we make them ours. We teach them to bend and contort and blow bubbles out of their trunks."

"Humans don't have trunks."

Nancy smiled. "No, sadly, they don't."

"Will that be good to do? And to watch?"

"We liked it when they all fell over. We all laughed and forgot how hungry and tired we were. There must be something to it. Something powerful. There must be."

"What can I do?"

"Think. What would you like from the humans? What would make you smile? Ask this of the others. Once we've all agreed on what we want the humans to do, we begin training."

Nancy hadn't noticed the other animals gathering around as she and Joe talked. But here they were. The horses and zebras, knee-deep in water. The giraffes, straining their necks to hear, the injured baboon standing tall and proud at the water's edge. The sheep were listening as they slowly chewed grass.

"Something about that seems fair," the zebra said.

"And we can still do whatever we want with them afterward," the giraffe said.

The other animals agreed. Nancy turned from Joe back toward the shore, toward the other animals, and she saw something new in her brethren. Purpose.

The training began. Nancy thought of Edgar and their days behind the whip. She missed him. The awareness brought back more sad memories than she wanted, and she forced herself to abandon them for the task at hand.

At first, the humans seemed relieved to be free of their bonds. They looked hopeful, perhaps expecting freedom. They still didn't speak, though they did communicate through smiles and eyes that grew bigger. But freedom did not come, and they realized that they were trading one set of bonds for another.

First they were taught to walk in a straight line, one after the other. They did somersaults on the ground. They ran in circles. They performed little dance steps. They jumped over each other, clumsily, and hit each other, and groaned. Joe and the baboon laughed. All the animals had met humans—acrobats, trapeze artists, gymnasts—whose bodies could do almost anything. They hadn't realized that these were such special talents.

Nancy made the humans climb on top of each other. They toppled over repeatedly until, after some practice, they perfected their pyramid. When they were all in place, the monkey ran up their legs and arms and placed a wreath of twigs and brush on the head of the highest human. Then he pushed her over, and the whole group of humans tumbled down. The animals roared with laughter. The monkey, who leapt onto a tree branch just as the collapse began, laughed hardest of all.

When Nancy ordered the humans to try the pyramid again, the young female walked toward her, on the balls of her feet, as though she was scared of making too much noise. She had mud stains on her knees. But she was smiling.

"That was fun," she whispered. Nancy pushed the girl away with her trunk, and the girl jumped back, almost losing her balance.

"Suzette, get back here!" the old female ordered. "I told you not to speak!"

The girl called Suzette backed away. Her face was contorted—sad and twisted.

"She looks like Babar," the girl said to anyone who would hear. Nancy had no idea what this meant.

Nancy, Joe, the monkey, and the baboon spent the next few hours training the humans to perform spins and turns and somersaults and handstands. The humans were quick studies. They didn't enjoy pain, the threat of being thrashed by the twigs the monkey had tied together kept them obedient.

When the humans seemed too tired, the animals let them rest and gave them water. They gave the humans oats to eat, but they didn't seem interested.

"They'll eat," said Nancy. "They'll have to, eventually."

By nightfall, the humans were ready. Joe and the monkey had cleared a small plot of land away from the shore, where the ground was firm and dry. Nancy stood in the background, thinking of cotton candy and salted pretzels. Just before the ringmaster had called her out to one of the three rings, her trainer would whisper words of false encouragement in her ears, and she would listen, eager to please, willing to perform even as the sounds of the crowds heightened her fear of failure. She could envision the light—how many times had it nearly blinded her as it beamed down from the rafters?

The show began. Not under the light of harsh bulbs, but the light of the moon and the stars. The oohs and aahs of the impatient crowd had been replaced by the gentle hum of the animals, shifting and breathing as they nestled in the soft cattails and prairie grass. And Nancy, the giant elephant, was no longer kneeling down, lying prostrate before the humans, awaiting her orders.

Instead, she was giving the orders. First, she had the humans pass around a ball of dried mud, using only their faces. After each pass, a mud stain would form on the foreheads, cheeks, and chins of the humans, which delighted the animals. Soon, Nancy couldn't tell the females from the males. Next, Nancy made the humans form their pyramid. The oldest male and one of the younger males stood at the base. The youngest male and the oldest female clumsily climbed on their shoulders. After the crouching humans had gained balance, the youngest female did her best to scale their bodies. She failed. She fell, and the rest of the pyramid collapsed. The old female went to console the girl, but the monkey slapped her away.

"How can they rule the planet?" the baboon asked.

Some of the humans formed hoops and others jumped through them, and the young girl, much to the delight of the animals, fell yet again. But she kept trying. She kept trying and failing. Finally, she was too hurt to try anymore. The female adult ran to her, this time ignoring the stings from the monkey's whip.

The baboon yawned. The others were still watching. But now the laughter came out not in unison, but slowly, like blood from a tiny puncture in the skin.

And when the humans used their heads and faces to volley the balls of mud, the laughter evaporated. The smaller humans had broken down. These humans were not talented. These were not the humans the animals had met at the circus. These slipped and fell. Their spirits broke quickly. Nancy looked at her friends. Some were sleeping. Some were bored. The baboon looked disgusted. She looked at the humans. They were shivering as night fell. The laughter had died.

Of course this wasn't working, Nancy thought. She needed fire or a trapeze artist. She needed clowns and men on stilts. Had she learned nothing in all her years in the circus? She needed to up the ante! She needed. Something.

She turned around looking for some prop, some vision that might inspire new tricks. But what she saw was the glint of two sad eyes, watching the performance from next to the bushes.

Nancy had forgotten about the tiger. But there he was. And in his searing eyes Nancy saw the pain she herself had felt when she had performed in the circus ring. That pain invaded her like a pestilence; it was as if she had replaced the humans in the clearing, as if they were watching her perform once more.

Then she knew. She knew.

There was nothing to learn here. Her plan hadn't worked.

She looked at the humans. She had never really looked at them before, not closely, not with pure curiosity or real interest. Now she saw their unhappiness. The fear and fury in the adults' eyes. The fright in the young boys'. The girl, however...the girl looked right back at Nancy, right into her eyes, and all Nancy saw was innocence. The girl saw Nancy looking at her. She broke formation and ran to her, put her hands on Nancy's trunk.

"Hello, Elephant," she said. "Are we doing everything right? Are you happy?"

The adults were calling her back—"Suzette, Suzette!"—but Nancy held on with her trunk, felt the smallness of the girl's being, the vulnerability. Nancy could kill her in a flash. She didn't. She pulled her ears back. She lowered her trunk. She wanted to cry, but instead she said, "Go back to your mother and father."

Suzette did as she was told.

Nancy rose and walked toward the humans. She nodded at the monkey, who unbound them.

"You're free to go," she said.

The human males tried to thank her but she hushed them with a swat of her trunk. The family didn't press her; they escaped swiftly into the night. Nancy never saw them again.

With the humans gone and the animals resting, Nancy was alone. Even Joe was sleeping. She wandered away from the makeshift circus toward nowhere. Maybe, she thought, she would emulate the humans and just disappear into the dark, cloudy night. She would migrate. She would find whatever it was she had lost.

Then she turned around and saw all the animals, their eyes shut, their mouths open, their breathing regular and calm, all of them dreaming of far-off places they would forget in the morning. They looked so vulnerable, innocent as the human girl. The thought struck her hard: These animals were hers. Their dreams, their fates, their lives. They trusted her to lead them. Had she been any different than the humans? How? She'd focused on what the circus had done to her; she'd thought only of *her* hurt. But the circus had pained them all, and through that pain they had formed a bond. She'd ignored that, and she'd wasted the responsibility they had placed in her.

"It's harder than we all imagined, isn't it?" she heard a voice say.

Nancy turned.

The tiger jumped down from a tree. He knew what was in her mind. It had been in his too.

Nancy smiled.

"Yes," she said quietly.

They sat together, silently, thinking about all that was wrong, all that was so very wrong with the world, and all that had to be done.

"No more hiding," he said. Nancy knew what he meant. They weren't so different, she thought.

"Anyway, you were right after all."

"About what?"

"About heading west. It's one thing to beat a few coyotes and peccaries. I wonder how the humans will stack up against a Bengal tiger and an African elephant?"

"I'm tired of wondering," Nancy said. "Of trying to solve this riddle."

"Being human is exhausting," the tiger said.

Nancy nodded. "No wonder they pair up."

They stared into the dark, momentarily lost in their thoughts.

"West, you say?" Nancy asked.

"Yes. Let's go west."

"To fight?"

"To fight the people who need to be fought against," the tiger said.

"And leave the rest alone," Nancy said.

"That," the tiger said, "is a good idea."

And then the canopy of stars and the full moon and the trickle of water and the beasts of north Texas were exactly where they were supposed to be.

Pig

323 was navigating the confusing expanse of the farm. Was awareness some form of madness, where the insanity manifested in subtle forms of trickery, pulling her this way, then that way, her mind full of ghosts and bones and dreams—all of which left her feeling split and exhausted? She'd been aware for less than one day and she was ready to surrender.

The other pigs were asleep. 323 could hear grunts and snores from all corners of the landscape as her former penmates stretched their legs out for the first time in their lives. Why couldn't she do the same?

The ferret walked alongside her. He also zigzagged, tripped, raced ahead, and walked right into her. He sang softly to himself: "Da-da-da, de-de-de, dum-de-dum-dum da."

"Where are you taking me?" 323 asked, out of breath. The ferret was wayward, but swift.

"To where it all begins."

"What does that mean? I'm tired. I don't understand the point of anything."

"It will all mean more once you see."

"Ferret. Quit speaking in riddles."

The ferret eyed her curiously. "You know, I'm new at words too. I'm new at knowing what the right thing to say or do is. I'm trying."

"I appreciate what you're doing," 323 said. "I just don't know what the point is. You said it earlier. They're going to win. I didn't want to believe it when you said it, but I do now, and frankly, I don't care. Even if we won, what sort of victory would it be? I'm a pig. What spoils can I hope for?"

The ferret looked up at 323. His face possessed a softness that 323 hadn't seen before.

"This is why I need to show you. I'm not good for anything. But the odd thing is, you are. I don't know why I know that." He scratched behind his ear. "The awareness floods our minds. But it doesn't change who any of us really are. And maybe..."

He scratched his ear again.

"Maybe?" 323 asked.

"Maybe, because of who you are—"

"Who I am? I'm a pig. Nothing more."

"I think you're more than that. Haven't you noticed that the other pigs began to listen to you almost as soon as you opened your mouth? The awareness didn't make you a great pig. It helped make the others recognize it. But there's more you need to know, to fully understand where you've been, and maybe, where you'll go. Me, I don't care anymore. But you—you will always care. You can't help it."

"I don't want to know more. And I don't want to care any more. It's been too much already," 323 protested.

But the ferret had already walked on and 323, without thinking, lumbered after him, still taking in the sights and sounds of the new world. Some of it was intoxicating, some of it too new to understand. And then there was that odd smell from the house, the smell that had made her stomach unhappy, that now seemed to be emanating from the ferret. It must be his drink, she thought.

The ferret led 323 along a concrete walk that eventually turned to a dirt path, lined with weeds and tufts of yellow grass and decayed flowers.

They were approaching another building. 323 could just make it out; it jutted up into the darkness, as large as her pen. The ferret slowed down his pace, much to 323's relief.

"This is it," he said, scratching that same itch behind his ears. Then he burped, covering his mouth with his dirty paw. "Sorry."

"What?" 323 asked.

"For that noise."

"No, I mean, what is this?"

"This is *it*." There was nothing extraordinary about the building at the surface. Still, something about it made her uneasy.

"I don't want to go in there." She backed off.

"But we must. We must go in there." The ferret circled her, as if in an effort to contain her.

"No, ferret. I'm done with this game. And that's what it is, a game. I don't care to win and I don't care to lose. One day has been enough."

The ferret's face fell. He sat down on the hard ground. "If there was ever time for a drink."

323 sat down beside him. She noticed that smell again.

"Why do you drink?"

"Well, it's only been for a day," the ferret said with a wry smile.

"I doubt it'll be just for today," 323 said.

"Yes, yes. This awareness is tricky. Some of us seem to have gotten more of it than others. Nature is never fair. I would just as soon give mine back." He paused. "And that's why I drink and you don't. Because I'm different."

"Of course you are," said 323, placating the small animal.

"No, no. Listen to what I'm saying. I'm *different*."

323 looked up at the moon and the stars and the dark spaces between them.

"I don't understand you, ferret."

"No one does. That's what I keep telling myself and it makes me feel better. It almost makes me happy. To be misunderstood. To be alone in the barn thinking about the boy who never loved me." The ferret stopped. He, too, watched the cinema of the night sky.

"It won't ever get old," he said.

"What?"

"Being able to put into words what the sky looks like. Dark and light and shining and empty all at once."

323 thought of herself standing in the silver halo of the human's gilt mirror. She shuddered.

"So, pig, what makes you different?" the ferret asked.

"I don't know. I became aware quickly. More quickly that the others. Or maybe I was always aware, and I just didn't know it. Maybe we all were. Maybe there's an awareness of awareness that has to come before awareness. Maybe..." But her words were twisting in her head and she couldn't finish her thought.

"Hmm. I could really use my thimble now," the ferret said, half to the pig, half to himself. "I'll go get it. Soon. But come on, we have work to do."

323 followed him to the building. In the dull light, she could see it was more like the barn than anything else. It seemed to have two stories but no windows, and its front door looked similar to the entrance to the pen.

"We have to get inside," the ferret said.

"Why would I want to get into another building? I don't care, ferret. I keep trying to tell you. I don't care."

The ferret laughed. "Let's just enter the building, then you can not care."

He sniffed around the perimeter of the building. "The door's locked, but maybe there's another way in."

"I'm going to go," 323 said. "I'm tired, ferret, and I want to sleep." She wanted to add "forever," but she stopped herself.

Just then, a deafening blast shook the land. Subsidiary coughs and hiccups followed the initial explosion.

323 and the ferret turned. From where they stood, they could see the human house lit up like an orange star, flames stretching from the windows, smoke waffling through the air, masking the previous stench with a new, decadent odor. Embers filtered through the darkness.

"I was in that house. Minutes ago." Shock reverberated through the pig. She could imagine the burning pictures, the burning mirror.

"So was I."

The ferret moved close. He and 323 watched the house burn down. They didn't speak.

"How did that happen?" 323 finally asked. "How, ferret? Are the humans back? Could they smell us in their domain? Are the other pigs safe? I have to go check on them."

The ferret smiled. "That is why I brought you here, 323."

The smell.

"What?" she said, distracted.

"Because you broke out of a jail, you walked through a graveyard, you escaped a house doomed for explosion, and here you are, worrying about something other than yourself."

"What's the smell, ferret? I smell something on your paws."

The ferret looked down at his feet. "Odd," he said. Then he looked back at the house. Small patches of fire started flickered up in their direction.

"It's kerosene, 323. Humans use it to burn things. I used it to burn things that were human."

"You did that?" 323 looked at the house.

"Yes," he said. "The house had to be destroyed. I had to do it."

323 didn't have time to argue. "This stuff is on your paws," she said. "I can smell it. You tracked it here. It's following us."

"That can't be."

"It is," said the pig. "It is." She looked back at the trail of fire. "We have to hurry, 323. Come, come now."

He scampered up and resumed looking for an entrance. 323 followed. The fire was spreading, from the house, through the grass, toward them.

"We have to get in there, 323. We have to. The fire has to stop. It wasn't supposed to come this way."

He's losing his mind, 323 thought.

"323, we have to get in."

"Why? Who cares if the building burns? It's a human building."

"No. It's not. Not inside."

The ferret ran to the front entrance. 323 followed.

She could smell something other than the kerosene here, a familiar scent.

"Ferret, are there pigs in there?"

"Pigs," the ferret said. "Pigs the humans left behind to die. Just like you. Pigs and pigs and pigs. But not like you."

"What do you mean?"

"There are pigs and there are pigs," the ferret said. "You'll see. Just get in there." He was taking quick breaths. "You're the only one who can save them. The humans left them to starve. You can bring them to life."

323 stepped back. She took a deep breath. If the ferret was right, and she suspected that he was, then she had to get in there. She couldn't let any other pig, any other mammal for that matter, suffer behind more closed, locked doors. She ran at full speed toward the door, ramming into it as hard as she could. Upon contact, she reeled backward and thudded to the ground.

She hadn't made a dent. She picked herself up and tried again.

Nothing.

Each time, after the pain in her shoulder receded, she turned, and each time, the fire was closer, its orange and yellow hues spilling forward, seeping closer. She listened for the pigs inside, for any sign other than the scent, but heard nothing.

Only the cheers of the ferret kept her charging. Again and again and again, she threw her weight into the door. After each defeat, she picked herself up.

The ferret was jittery, talking to himself, cursing the air.

On her eighth attempt, the door cracked. Her shoulders throbbed with the blushing softness of a fresh bruise. She didn't care. She was inside. The ferret was close behind her.

She squealed in victory.

"I knew you could do it," he said.

She barely heard him. She was still focused on the door, reveling silently as she stared down at the jagged wood and the loose copper bolts. But her victory over the door was short-lived.

She looked up and saw cages. Cages and cages. A large pen filled with nothing but iron cages barely bigger than the pigs they held.

A room of pigs in cages.

She closed her eyes because she didn't want to see. She closed her eyes and thought of the fake life that had seemed so real in the mirror, a mirror that was now cracked and burning quicksilver, reflecting nothing. Everything was shattered or burning. 323 shrank down. Maybe if she kept her eyes shut, she could imagine it all away and shrink into a dark womb of her own making.

"We are running out of time," the ferret said.

"We?" 323 bellowed. "We?" She was breathing hard. She opened her eyes and took in the room once more. Inside the cages, grotesquely large pigs with swollen teats opened their mouths, drool draining off of their jowls. 323 went up to one of these pigs and rubbed her head against its exposed belly. The pig jumped, shocked by the sensation of skin on skin. The pig tried to lift her head, but couldn't.

323 began whispering to the pig. They were okay, she repeated, they would be okay. As she spoke, she studied the cages, seeking some weakness. How could she get in? And how would she get the pigs out?

She scanned the locks. She jiggled them with her nose. Then, she let her eyes roam the large room. There were at least twenty more cages, at least twenty more pigs, lost to lethargy inside their locked worlds.

She turned and looked outside.

"Can we stop the fire?" she asked the ferret, though of course she knew the answer.

"No," he said.

"I can't get into these locks. And the cages are made of steel. I can't just knock them down like the door."

"Keys," said the ferret. "There must be keys. I remember the boy used keys to lock his bicycle. They open things. Keys."

"Go and find them then. In a shed maybe?"

The ferret nodded and ran off into the blazing night.

The fire was coming closer.

323 turned back, nudging the pig again. The pig moaned, a low, guttural sound that reverberated through the dirt floor.

"I'm here," 323 said.

The pig's eyes shone like onyx discs in the vague light of the impending flames. She blinked. She opened her mouth, but no words came out.

"Are you aware?"

"Yes," the pig said, finally. She lifted her head, then dropped it, letting out another low groan.

"I'm here. Do you need water?"

"No," the pig said. "Let us die."

"Why are you in here? Why haven't I seen you in the pen?"

The pig snorted out a painful, unhappy laugh.

"You have seen me."

"I haven't."

"Put your snout through the slats. Feel my belly again."

This sentence, with its many words, tired the pig. She was short of breath.

323 did as the other pig asked. The belly was tight, swollen.

"Your belly. It's heavy with offspring."

"This is what I do."

She felt herself nodding at the pig's words. She understood. She looked around. Every pig in every cage was bloated with progeny.

"We are due to deliver soon. It would be better for the piglets if we just die first. All of you are our children. No one knows who's the mother of whom. We give birth, and then we give birth again. I could be your mother. I could be anyone's mother."

Again, the pig moaned. This time the sound was so deep that dust from the floor floated up into the fluorescence of the fiery sky.

323 looked around in desperation. She had to free these pigs. She attacked one of the locks with her teeth. But the metal didn't give. Where was the ferret? She called out to him.

He was looking for keys, she remembered. She had little faith he would find them. But it seemed to be their only hope.

The pigs in the cages felt the fire approaching. But their spirits were too broken to care. Besides, 323 thought, what could they do?

"Think," 323 said to herself. Think. She looked around, and around, until she'd made herself dizzy.

Think. Let the awareness in. *Think*. She closed her eyes.

She opened them. The cages were locked, yes, but each was locked by a single connecting tube—a copper tube that journeyed from one end of the barn to the other. Why was that? What did that copper tube do?

She closed her eyes again. Think.

Electricity! The word was new to her, but like so many others, she grasped it. She rolled it around in her mind until the concept was clear. Was this tube electric? If so, how to make it non-electric? She didn't know. She followed the tube to the end of the room. There it connected to machinery.

The fire was getting closer.

No, the tube wasn't electric. It was a pump of some sort. It was air pressure. Pistons at the end. Copper tubing with brass fittings at each section. If she could puncture the tubing, she could release the air pressure. And the locks would open. Wouldn't they?

But how? How could she do this?

"Think," she said to herself again. Think. She tried biting the tube, but her teeth weren't strong enough to pierce it.

She could feel the fire coming closer. The night was beginning to warm into a kind of day, the sky glowing orange. The other pigs could see it. But they didn't care.

"Think," she said aloud.

She scanned the room. She thought about the awareness. What was the first thing she had become aware of? She looked down. Her hooves. Yes. Those hard hooves, harder than the rest of her, seemingly made of bone.

She took her two front hooves and, like a stallion, reared up on on her hind legs and then crashed forward into the copper piping.

It gave a little. Not enough. But a little. She knew. She knew. She reared back and did it again. And again. Each time, the copper gave way. Now the final attack. Yes. She had punctured the copper, she could hear air seeping through. The pressure in the pipes was decreasing then, wasn't it? Yes. Decreasing, decreasing until...whoosh...the locks switched open. The pigs were free.

But they didn't move.

"Open your doors," 323 shouted. She ran through the aisle between the cages. "The doors aren't locked. Open your doors and run out! Run!"

But the pigs just looked at her.

Finally, one of them spoke. "I haven't used my legs in years."

"I've never used my legs," another said.

"Tonight you will. Just push the door open with your snout, and come."

323 raced around the confines, urging the entrapped pigs to rise.

At first the pigs refused to budge. And perhaps, if the fire hadn't been encroaching, they never would have. But finally, the threat of the fire was enough. The pigs struggled. Their legs were weak and their bodies too big. Still, they found a way to stand. Their back lifted the metal lids. The fat of their sides leaked out of the slats. Their short legs churned. As the flames began to lick the barn, as the walls became flint for the impending inferno, the pigs, escaping from sheaths of metal, inched their way through the front door. 323 shouted at them, she encouraged them. And they made it out. All of them found a way out.

The ferret appeared, running. "No keys," he shouted, but then he saw the pigs outside, safe. Soon many of the pigs from the pen, awoken by the explosion and the fire, had joined them. Here were their mothers, they learned, and they nudged each other, and talked, and sniffed, and wondered who belonged to whom, and why that suddenly seemed to matter. They moved away from the burning building to the safety of a close-by meadow, sultry from the fire's heat but also cooled by the evening temperature.

323 stayed by the birthing pigs throughout the night. They watched the fire burn down to nothing. They spoke of their next round of piglets, how they'd be born into something different than any of the rest of them. Some were fearful. Most were hopeful. They thanked 323, over and over. She thanked them back. The other pigs asked her how she did it, how she was able to free the birthing pigs.

"I used my mind," she said. "My body. And my hooves." They all looked at their own bodies and hooves, and wondered what they would have done. Then they asked her to tell the story again and again. She might never have the kind of family she dreamed of in the house, but she felt she was getting something like it out here in the meadow.

Soon, the birthing pigs felt the fresh morning air for the first time. 323 watched as they tested themselves against the new elements, using their legs to walk for the first time, eating the food that the other pigs brought them, sniffing the ground, smelling the grass, coming to life. Currents of dust and debris swirled in the ashen air, rising up from somewhere unseen, waiting as the smoky dawn approached.

Dog

Why is my name Cooper?

They'd been waiting. For another noise, a scream, a car revving. Anything that would give them a sense that life was continuing outside. But they heard nothing. They sat quietly, each sinking deeper into his or her own thoughts.

Cooper. He had never thought about what it meant to have a name. Why Cooper? He rested his face on his paws, his eyes fluttering open when the others sighed or spoke. With Larry and Mary Lee gone, the tension that had charged the basement diffused, and Cooper could at least pretend it was a stable environment, a place where he could rest. But he couldn't stop thinking.

He thought of his name, silently repeating the word. *Cooper.* The sound seemed as inexorable a part of him as his fur, or his love of the chase, his need to be praised. But maybe it was nothing more than a random group of syllables that labeled him? He understood now that humans gave names to everything—to their babies, their pets.

He opened, then raised an eye. Carol was shifting uncomfortably. *Cooper.* He was beginning to resent it—the name that Jessie squealed when he licked her face into submission, the name that branded his tags and jingled each time he moved. Could he be both a mammal going off to war *and* a pet named Cooper?

"Cooper, what are you thinking?" Jessie asked.

"Nothing."

Jessie didn't press him. She knew him, though; she probably knew he was lying.

"Why did you name me Cooper?" he finally asked.

Jessie shook her head. "What a strange question. Cooper was the name of the first boy I had a crush on. Years ago.

In elementary school. I always liked the name. I guess you reminded me of him somehow."

"You named me after a school girl crush?"

Jessie shrugged. "So? It's a good name. It suits you. It always did."

His name—that sound that seemed so crucial to his identity—was nothing but a nostalgic whim.

They think only of themselves. He sighed. The room had calmed, but this was no sanctuary; he couldn't sit here and feign rest. He walked without wagging his tail. He kept his eyes down. He thought about the times when Jessie locked him in the apartment when she went outside, the times she forgot to feed him, the moments he needed love and she wasn't there, too busy with the comings and goings of her job and her boyfriends and Peter. Baths. Flea collars. The severe slaps when he had an "accident."

He felt angry. The anger flowed both from and into the revolution. They were all angry. He sat back down, wrapping his tail around his legs. For one brief moment, he let himself imagine it. Taste a human. Tear into it. Isn't that what the rats had urged? Rip it from the bone and tendon, gnaw at the sinews and dig until the marrow bursts forth. He found himself rising, walking slowly toward Carol, who was fiddling with the dead radio. If he just took one bite, other bites would follow, each would be easier than the first, each would satisfy this new hunger—a hunger that was more powerful and primal than the name of some third-grade tow-headed boy, this hunger that belonged only to him.

How terrible it was to be tame! He took another step. Then one more. And this is how the bites would go, one and then another, and then another.

He walked around and around the basement, an animal chasing his own thoughts.

He sat again, and, for a while, there was quiet. He'd wait. He'd think.

Then the door at the top of the stairs jerked open, hitting the wall with a loud thud.

The bats, he thought, but he was wrong.

An animal stood in the entrance. He was grey and black, with pointed ears and a long snout. His delicate nose twitched as it tried to find something familiar in the squalid air.

"Wolf," Cooper whispered.

Carol scudded back toward the wall. Jessie stared, motionless. The wolf lifted his head and beamed his yellow gaze at the room below. The iridescent eyes, the matted fur, the clotted blood along his neck, the mud that ringed his large, flat paws all were signs of a powerful war-torn being. The wolf let out a tremendous yowl. Carol trembled. Jessie took a few steps back. Cooper wanted to run toward the ancient animal and run away from it at once. For a moment he was sure the wolf's roar was meant solely for him, a trumpet to action, a reminder of his true identity.

The wolf took a step. Then he leapt from the top of the stairs to the bottom in two beautiful bounds. Cooper could smell the scent of death on him. It was sharp, it made Cooper's mouth water. Take Carol," Cooper said to himself. Take Carol. He tried to push the wolf towards her, but the wolf didn't have any interest in hunting the weak and wounded. He silently stalked the room. Jessie, Carol, and Cooper might as well have grown roots in the cement floor.

The wolf snorted, then bared his teeth and yowled again. Carol shrieked, her body collapsing in fear. Jessie ran to her.

These sudden movements stoked the wolf to attack. Cooper watched the animal retract onto his back feet, then thrust his body forward, cutting through the air with an acrobat's ease.

Cooper couldn't stop himself. He lunged at the wolf, meeting him in midair, striking. The wolf was focused on Jessie's gullet, and Cooper had no trouble making contact with a crimson wound along the wolf's neck. Cooper bit into it with all of his strength until his body and the wolf's were tangled into one.

He could taste foreign blood, maybe Larry's, maybe another person's, and then the blood of the wolf. It was salty, vital, repulsive. The wolf yelped. He fell to the floor, writhing. Cooper rolled on top of him, then jumped up. The wolf, whimpering, stayed down.

"Kill it, Cooper!" Carol yelled.

Jessie narrowed her eyes at the grounded wolf.

"Kill it!" Carol screamed again.

It was the only thing to do. Cooper gnashed his teeth. He would do it, finish it, finish this.

But hadn't he told himself the same thing earlier?

Would this ever be over?

He looked at Jessie. She looked at him.

The wolf was losing blood. It flowed from his neck, a small red river with a pulsing current. He was too weak to fight now; for a wolf, not fighting was tantamount to death. He closed his yellow eyes with an impotent flutter of his lids. Still, Cooper couldn't take the final breath from the grey animal, his ancestor. He stood, staring at the beast who lay sprawled before him, muddled and scarred from battle.

"I can't," Cooper said. "I can't kill him."

The wolf attempted to rise. Cooper steadied himself, instinctively readying himself to attack. He couldn't kill the wolf, but he couldn't allow Jessie to be killed either. The wolf struggled up, zigzagging across the room like an old wind-up toy running down. Cooper followed. When it became clear the wolf was just wobbling around the basement on the fumes of pride and honor, Cooper guided him into the third room. He needed to segregate the two beings that were fighting for his loyalty, the two species who seemed most like his family—wolf and human.

The dazed animal circled the little room, searching for a nest, an enemy, a purpose—something.

Cooper needed to kill him. It wasn't fair to let him die this way, slowly, painfully, an evaporating shadow.

The wolf collapsed onto a dusty knit rug.

A simple tear of the jugular and the wolf would be dead. Cooper walked up to him, his head lowered in reverence, and sniffed the wound he'd helped to open.

"I just can't kill you," Cooper whispered.

"I can," said a soft, knowing voice from above.

Clio perched on a high shelf. She dropped gracefully to the ground and, with a quick, feral pounce, she was on the wolf, gnawing on his neck, ending his life.

The wolf didn't fight.

Cooper looked away. He would sooner look at anything other than a domestic cat opening the arteries and destroying the essence of a wolf. A poster on the wall showed a large-breasted woman in sunglasses opening a beer bottle. On the poster next to it a shortstop froze midair, mid-throw. Clio walked right under Cooper's nose so that he could smell the remnants of the wolf on her breath, in her whiskers.

"We have to leave now," she said. "Someone will know the wolf is missing. Perhaps they'll guess we did it. And even if they don't know, we do."

Cooper hated this room. He took a few heavy steps back, stumbling on the bodies of two rats, freshly dead, fang marks in their necks.

Cooper looked at Clio.

Clio looked down at the ground. "Dogs aren't the only animals who know how to love," she said quietly, and then walked to
the room where Carol and Jessie sat, still in shock after the wolf
attack. Cooper followed.

"Clio," Jessie cried, grabbing the cat and holding her close,
nearly smothering her. "Oh, Clio," she murmured. "My darling
Clio." Cooper remembered when Jessie brought Clio home from
the shelter. The tiny kitten was nervous, she hid in the corners
and looked out at the world through glinting, suspicious eyes.
Her short life had been punctuated by alley fights and pigeon
wars, and already she'd possessed a defiant if grave personality.
Cooper wished he could enjoy the sight of her now, relaxed and
purring in Jessie's arms, but he could still feel the presence of
the dead wolf, the dead rats, in the other room. His head ached.

Clio wriggled out of Jessie's grasp.

"It's time we left," she said.

"But you just got here, Clio," Jessie argued.

"I've been here the whole time," Clio stated calmly. She
didn't tell Jessie what Cooper now realized: The cat had hidden
herself away because she knew that she'd have fallen into the
dog's predicament: the inability to chose sides.

"But I have so much I want to ask you, so much I need to ask
you..."

"You were wonderful," Clio cut Jessie off. "That's all you
need to know. We have to *go*."

"No," Jessie said.

"Clio's right," Cooper said. "It's not safe here. Not for Clio.
Not for me. And it's not safe for you if we stay here."

"So you will fight," Jessie said tentatively.

"Yes," Clio said.

"We're enemies now, aren't we," Jessie murmured, the
words stepping from her mouth with slow precision.

"No," Cooper said. He would go off his way, Jessie hers; that didn't make them enemies. He and Clio began to walk up the stairs. Jessie stifled a cry, but Cooper didn't turn. He and Clio were on their way.

But then the door flung open once again. This time no bat or wolf confronted them. This time it was a wounded, bloodied, raving man, with curled fingers gripping a woodman's axe.

"She's dead and I was left for dead," Larry said. He swung the axe at Cooper, who ducked, avoiding the metal edge.

"Larry, no!" Jessie screamed. But Larry swung again. This time Cooper was ready. This time he didn't have to stop himself from attacking, didn't have to worry if he was attacking friend or foe; that switch in his brain that had been oscillating between right and wrong, human and mammal, pet and slave, didn't apply to Larry.

His jaw found the sweet spot in Larry's hand, his teeth snapping around the phalanges. The axe dropped to the floor. Cooper attacked Larry's face, working over the human's senses with a series of vicious scratches.

Larry fell to the floor. He gasped for breath. He reached out and pointed a finger at Jessie. Cooper bore into him relentlessly until the finger lay in repose, pointing at nothing except the stifling air.

Cooper panted. He could hear things he hadn't before. A buzz of bees, the subtle fervor of rustling wind, the faint purr of a prideful house cat. With Larry dead, with the taste of that victory leading him, he left the human carcass, stepping over the hardening waste, rubbing his paws into the fleshy recesses between the ribs.

Jessie was crying. Cooper had forgotten how easily humans wept. He watched her. He had wondered what it was like to be human at the onset of the awareness and now he understood at least one nuance of the human condition. To spare a weaker entity seemed to him to be the highest form of awareness.

Jessie drew back as he approached her. With his eyes and his demeanor he let her know that she wouldn't be harmed. She quickly realized this and drew toward him, holding her face in his fur, letting the tears drip on his body. He looked over at Carol, who was holding a knife she must have discovered somewhere in the toolbox under the table. It looked like her, rusty and tough and used.

Where did he belong? He looked up the stairs, where Clio was waiting. Then he turned to Jessie. He had made up his mind. But once again he was interrupted.

"Any and all humans, make your way out of your houses," a metallic voice boomed from outside. "We have an armed bus to take you to shelter. You must come out now. You must board the bus. You must join us."

"Praise God," Carol moaned, crossing herself.

"Come with me, Jessie. They're here. Run."

She darted up the stairs, surprising everyone with her sudden energy, the energy of boundless relief.

"Mom!" Jessie ran after her. Cooper and Clio followed. Soon they were all outside, on the front porch, in the quiet twilight of a summer evening.

A man emerged from a large yellow bus with flashing red lights. He looked like any number of men Cooper had seen delivering food, picking up garbage cans, dropping off packages, except that his body was covered in thick, protective clothing and he wore a strange helmet. He yelled something to Carol and Jessie, something that Cooper couldn't hear.

"What?" Jessie yelled

The man started waving at the two women frantically, then pulled something from the back of his pants, something that shone in the bland light of a sun just set.

"There are two beasts behind you," the man screamed. "Get out of the way!" Then he aimed the shining object—a gun, Cooper could see now that it was a gun—at Cooper, the more deadly of the two beasts.

Cooper cocked his head. Jessie was screaming at the man, waving her arms at him.

Above, Cooper could hear the faint conversation of two plovers perched on a juniper branch.

The gun flashed in the man's hand. Cooper needed to run, but he was frozen by the artistry and the power of that glinting object. All the indecision of the day, the sense of being pulled back and forth, drifted away, the tension in his mind and his heart relaxing. Let it be, he thought. Let it be.

The gun fired. He felt nothing. But he heard a gasp, and then a moan. He opened his eyes and saw blood spilling from a body. For a second he was confused—Jessie?

It was Carol. She had leaned between Cooper and the bullet; she had shielded him with her body, saved his life just as he had saved hers. The bullet had slammed into her chest.

"Mom!" Jessie screamed, leaning over her Carol's body. "You shot her!" she shouted at the man.

Carol was bleeding badly. She choked, and looked at Cooper. In her eyes he saw a wisdom, a kindness, he had never seen before. "You run now," she said. "It doesn't matter what you want, what you think. You just run."

He ran. The man wasn't going to take the chance he'd hit another human, so he let the gun slump by his side. Jessie was gathering her mother up and helping her walk to the bus.

Another woman from inside the vehicle had come out to help as well.

Cooper sprinted behind the junipers under the watchful eyes of the plovers and the bored, rising moon. The evening had come and with it the ancient sounds and shadows.

Jessie and the other woman helped Carol limp to the bus, which was full of curious, frightened humans trying to comprehend what had just happened. They had seen so much that this was just another incident in a day that had dawned badly.

As Cooper approached the trees behind the house, Clio emerged from behind a small evergreen. "Let's leave," she said.

But Cooper couldn't stop staring at the bus. He had a clear view of its side, and he could see Jessie's face pressed up against a window, her eyes frantically searching.

Cooper stared until she spotted him, until she put her hand up to the window of the bus, which was beginning to pull away. Her tears clouded the glass.

He nodded. "I'll find you," he called. "I will find you again!"

But Jessie was gone now, and the yellow bus drove down the road, puffs of exhaust escaping in angry bursts until it disappeared down another street.

Bear

After he watched the human go, after he traveled past battles, past human after human and mammal after mammal, after the armies moved on to distant fields and pastures and cities, after the summer had ebbed away and the green leaves turned brown and brittle, the bear decided he'd observed all he could. He felt he could never be more aware.

The word "creation." It haunted him. He needed to understand it, and the only way to do that was to move. Words were meaningless in isolation and in theory. All summer he had sat in his cave, thinking, watching, wandering outside for food, lying in the sun, returning to his cave. He saw equations in the forest lines, he calculated the geometry of the sky, he sought refuge in the mathematics of his new awareness.

The world had changed. The landscape around him seemed empty. The awareness had driven most of the animals to the fronts. But I can't do this alone, he thought. He had always enjoyed his solitary life, but if he wanted to thrive, to experiment, to discover what awareness truly meant—if he wanted to create, he needed others. He had it in his mind to create a place where he and others could work and thrive together, where they could use their awareness, make it mean something. Something important.

He left the cave for good. When the urge to turn and retreat back to his home overwhelmed him, he reminded himself that his fear was normal. He'd lived the way bears had always lived. But awareness meant abandoning the way of the bear.

"I'm fine," he whispered to himself as he traversed a ravine and through a wide strawberry patch. The berries had long since ripened. Still, he hunted for remnants, his mouth watering. He moved on to a small treeless plain sheltered by mountains and forest, and considered making it his camp. But there was no water, and he moved on. Each step took him further from everything he had known.

He walked and walked. Over a small mountain, past a beehive, underneath watching birds, through fields still buzzing with insects mating before the coming frost. He detected animals as he traveled, but he didn't bother them.

He came across an expanse of wild grass. Magenta flowers leaned back toward the ground, heavy with autumn. Clouds scraped nervously along the sky. A small brook wound around the periphery.

This was the place. A sense of warmth entered his body and settled nicely in his bones.

He began exploring and came across the faint scent of another bear who had probably gone off to war long ago. He found a neighboring lea, not near enough to the brook, plagued by catchweed and clover and something else too. Besides weeds, the lea held the embers of man and animal. The bear sat down, closing his eyes as the wind pushed up the ghosts the earth had swallowed.

"We are better than this," he said aloud.

"Are we?" A hare had snuck up behind him. "Are we better than this?"

The bear looked down at the small animal.

"Do I know you?"

"Does that matter?" The hare did not take his eyes off the field.

"I held a hare in my hands when this began. It seems like so long ago..."

"It wasn't me," the hare said.

The bear sighed.

"I wish that this world was different," he said simply.

"The world is the way the world is," the hare said. "It's a very simple world, really. You live and then you die. Every action seems so important in between those basic steps. They're not."

"I will make the world different," the bear said. "Come with me, hare. Come with me to this little stretch of land. We can live there together. You and I."

"I need burrows. I need to be hidden. A field?" The hare laughed.

"Maybe you wouldn't need that. Maybe I could protect you?"

The hare just stared at him. The bear rose and walked away. Before he entered the forest he turned, "I hope I see you again, hare."

But the hare was gone.

The bear said to himself: "Basic steps."

He took his next step—he needed to find animals who had avoided the fighting. This wasn't easy. Most behaved like the hare, too concerned with surviving than following the words of the bear. A hyperactive marmot labeled him crazy. An injured fox found him arrogant. A lost prairie dog couldn't understand what the bear was talking about. After each encounter, the bear thanked them and moved on.

Eventually, he stumbled across a group of sturdy beavers. He told them of his plans to build something new, a place where any creature would be welcome. The beavers shielded their eyes from the waning sun as they looked up at the bear. They seemed in awe of his size and stature, of his commanding voice and words. They listened and nodded.

"Let's begin," he said.

They began gnawing wood, shaping it and then stacking it at a fork in the brook. The bear tried to learn from them, to help them. But his paws were too large. He fumbled and dropped things. The beavers grew impatient.

"Maybe there's another way," they said.

"Yes," the bear agreed. "We can all live in a cave. Or just out in the open. Or in a tree."

"No," the beavers argued. "*We* can't."

"I don't know what to do then," the bear admitted.

"Why are you doing this at all?" one of the beavers asked. "Why not just fight? Why don't you follow the army? Kill what needs to be killed."

"I can't," was all the bear could say. Then he added, "Why don't you all go and fight?"

"We lost five members of our family in one hour of warfare. That was enough for us." The beavers dropped their heads reverently for a few moments. One of the beavers finally broke the silence.

"We fear we are cowards. But we had to quit before we perished." Another added, "We have to get ready for winter. That's what we do. If not us, who will?"

The bear nodded. His winter was coming too.

So they continued to erect a structure next to the brook. They did the best they could. The bear thought about his answer—"I can't"—as the animals toiled together in the cool autumn afternoon.

Some day he would need a better answer. In the meantime, he focused on his work, watching the beavers chisel down the wood and flatten the mud, molding it into the appropriate shape and size. He watched with the wonder of a child at the building of a temple.

One afternoon, as the bear gathered wood for the beavers, a porcupine appeared. "What are you doing here?" the small creature asked.

"I'm building a safe place for everyone to live."

"Everyone?"

"Every animal who desires to be here," the bear said He reached down and carefully touched the daggers on the animal's back. The porcupine recoiled into a ball.

"But who among us can live under a beaver's dam?" the creature asked, and then, as he uncoiled and shuffled off into the forest thicket, he answered his own question. "Only a beaver."

"Where would you like to live?" the bear called out.

The porcupine stopped. "I'd prefer the hollow of a tree."

"Wouldn't you get lonely there?"

"I know my loneliness well. We wear each other comfortably."

"Am I a fool?" the bear asked the porcupine.

"Who's to say who's a fool and who's a genius? Just don't forget to be a bear."

So the bear left the beavers and their dam. Politely, they asked him why he was going, and he said because he needed to move, because he would crush their work with his size and weight. The beavers and the bear waved goodbye, and they touched each other as humans did.

The bear traveled south. He spent the next days alone. He stared into the sky. He slept for long periods and in that sleep he saw things that shook him awake, flashes of brilliant light, a sea that was calm and blue, meeting places where soft conversations were spoken by indistinguishable figures, a sky full of migrating birds. He figured they were portents, and that they mattered, but they were just out of reach, like his mother, like his understanding of humans or his need to do whatever it was he was doing.

He decided to stay awake from sunset to sunrise. He met animals he'd never seen before. Tall birds with mammalian traits. Domesticated animals who knew the tyranny—and the love—of the human. Spirited sea mammals who swam close to the shore and blew water from holes. He saw the scars of the revolution on many of these animals—scars in their skin and fur; scars in their shaky paws, their quiet minds. He wished he could ignore these signs of death and destruction, the memories they evoked of scorched land and scorched soldiers.

He learned to slow his mind as he traveled south. In those first few hours of awareness thoughts had come in wave after wave, but his need to understand his awareness abated now, its formerly deafening fervor a soft hum.

Somewhere between the ocean and the forest, he stumbled across an empty human town. It was just past twilight when he found the main street. A strange yellow light flickered from the bulbs overhead. Empty storefronts and tattered homes were like patchy fur lining the street. He could imagine these humans, here in their caves and dens, their nests and houses. He found the locks and gates and hedges amusing.

They build everything up to keep everyone out, he thought. They create these endless towns, cities. They had thrived here only recently. Now nothing but vacancy remained.

The bear sat down on the curb. The hardness of the concrete pleased him.

He would stay here. He would live like the humans, in their buildings, enshrouded by their warm walls and tiled roofs. Why not? Why not see what these shelters had to offer? Why not use them to create something new?

Wandering down the street, he found an enormous building, a store, with a large sign featuring symbols and a star. He entered through the unlocked door and sifted through the endless aisles, through the showy merchandise of the human empire. He marveled at the sheer volume, at the variety of invention. And though his brain now knew the words for these human creations, he didn't care to recall them. He just wanted to stare at these objects, then turn and rest for the night. And so he curled up in a corner where the humans had created an ersatz beach, with sand and colored balls that slowly shrank in size.

In the morning, he went outside. A light drizzle was falling. He lifted his paws up and felt the feathery wetness, and it felt good.

"What are you doing?" asked a squirrel. He had been watching the bear from a nearby tree branch.

"I'm enjoying the rain." The bear kept his arms raised, his eyes closed.

"No, I mean what are you doing here?"

"I don't know. And I don't care. Nor should you. Frankly, I've heard enough from small creatures," the bear said.

"Okay." The squirrel shrugged, then he scurried off the branch and down the tree trunk. He closed his small eyes and lifted his arms up to the sky. Just like the bear.

"This is better than war," said the bear.

The squirrel opened his eyes and dropped his arms.

"Why did you have to bring that up?"

"Bring what up?"

"The revolution."

"Am I not allowed?"

"Do you not know what's happening?"

"No, I don't. But I don't care. Come inside. I found something you might think interesting."

"I won't go in there."

"Why?"

"It has human residue."

"Does that matter?"

"Those walls were built on our backs."

"How so?"

The squirrel pondered this question, and then shook his head, "I don't know."

"Just come inside."

"No."

"We don't need to fear them."

"You've never had to fear anything, bear. I have. Fear is important. It reminds us what we can and can't do."

"Come inside. Sit with me. Tell me more about fear. I seem to be the type of mammal to whom small mammals tell their hardships. Talk to me. I have food for you. And a warm place to rest."

The squirrel considered this.

"I suppose it wouldn't hurt."

Inside, the bear tore open a package of salted nuts for the squirrel. They sat quietly in a tiled aisle and swapped stories of war and life before. The squirrel had participated in an attack led by badgers that had pushed the humans out of a small western city. The fighting had been brutal, the humans launching a counterattack using arms, chemicals, fire.

"It sounds like a great battle," the bear said.

The squirrel cracked a nut in his mouth.

"I am not sure, but I think we won."

After a few days, the abandoned store began to seem exactly like what the bear had set out to build so many weeks prior. He and the squirrel lived under the fluorescent lights that shone a waxy, sterile light on their fur. They broke open the windows so that the air could whip through freely. They drank water and tasted soda. They ate fruit the humans would have deemed rotten.

Every so often remote, earthshaking noises jarred both animals. But the noises eventually stopped, and the bear and the squirrel carried on. One day a weary and wounded cat wandered in, half-starved, and the bear and the squirrel fed her so much she quickly became fat. A dark-eyed, war-ravaged raccoon made a home in the hardware section. A few other animals arrived, some healthy, some starved, some driven half-crazy by war. A weasel stepped through the sliding glass doors, smiling to see what his future held, and died on the spot.

One day, the bear slipped on a puddle of water that had formed after a heavy rain battered the store. He tried to grab onto a rack of winter coats, but he was too heavy, and both bear and coats hit the floor with a loud thud. The squirrel and the cat laughed, and then the bear laughed. The bear laughed so hard that his rumbles rustled the branches of the snow-laden trees outside. The cat laughed so hard she cried; she had to stop laughing eventually because her stomach hurt. But the bear kept on.

And it was as if that laughter had wings, as if that laughter had taken on an odd corporeality. It sprang into the wind like a child in need of an embrace and twisted in the late autumn cold. The laughter comforted mammals who felt that cold as they never had before. It was as if their new mental awareness had heightened their awareness of their bodies. They had discovered discomfort. Many felt the sting of death. Many felt the first pangs of adolescent letdown at the realization that life and time will always win. Many hated war. But as they heard the laughter sweeping the air, they stopped shivering for a few brief moments, they forgot the dead, they remembered that time hadn't beaten them just yet and that there was a sun, bright and steady, waiting behind a cloud, resting before its ascension.

The laughter slowed, stilling into silence. But remnants were kept alive by a chain of animals who wouldn't let the laughter die, who spread it from mountain to meadow. One whispered to another, "Did you hear about the bear who can laugh louder than thunder?"

"Did you hear about the bear who lives where the humans lived?"

"Did you hear about the bear who doesn't fight?"

Some mammals hated to hear talk of this bear; they didn't believe in him or the stories attached to him. Laughter is not thunder. No one had *really* heard any laughter.

But a few wanted to believe. A network of sorts formed by accident—animals who had tired of the war, or whose awareness had now settled into their souls, who wanted something different from it than rage or vengeance. These animals pointed the way. Go west, they said, or east, or north. Just go. And a few more animals listened, and believed, and began an exodus from their burrows and nests, from the fronts and the battles in the interminable revolution, in order to seek out the bear.

When the new arrivals joined him, the bear saw their skepticism and sensed their weariness. "Come," he'd say. "Sit." And the animals would. The squirrel, the cat, the raccoon, and the others would bring food and drink. And the bear would shrink down as low as he could and ask the animals about their journeys, the troubles they had witnessed on the road. Sometimes, because of something the bear or perhaps the cat or the squirrel had said, someone laughed. When the newcomers heard that oddly familiar laughter they began to believe that this was a better place than the last.

It didn't take long for the animals who came to the bear to thrive in the human ruins. Overhead, owls and magpies and hawks circled, watching. The birds retained their mystery.

In the background booms rang out. But the animals grew to ignore the din. They began to shed their need to sniff the air, to feel the currents, to mark a territory.

And then one night something happened, and when it did, it seemed as though this animal village had been secretly awaiting, silently fearing, this very moment.

A human appeared at the door of the converted store. An adult male. He had no shirt and his pink skin was blotched where the sun had struck him, his neck and back scratched where animals had torn into him. He was skeletal. His face was sunken with hunger, drained by thirst. His blue eyes darted around the storefront.

The animals who'd been busy preparing the evening meal stopped. The animals who napped during the early evening awoke. The animals who chipped or yawned or played with stones ceased those activities and focused on the withered being who had stumbled into their home.

The human was breathing hard. He tried to move back through the entrance, but something unseen pushed him toward the dozens of curious eyes lingering upon him.

The bear, who had been conversing with two stallions about the great mountains in western America, scanned the large room, sensing the change in mood. When he spotted the human, he did what he always did when he saw a newcomer. He went to greet him.

"Come. Sit."

But the other animals didn't crowd around the newcomer as they usually did. They didn't strain their ears to hear his tales of war and peace. The bear clenched his jaw. He looked down at the cowering human. "Tell us how you arrived here."

One of the horses had followed the bear. "Who cares how he got here?" he asked.

The bear turned. "I do." He turned back to the human. "What do you need? We have food and drink."

The horse glowered behind the bear's back. The human continued to dart his eyes from animal to animal. He opened his mouth, but no sound emerged.

"It's okay. No one will hurt you."

And the bear's tone made it known to everyone in the room that his statement was a fact.

"Things are bad," the human said. "I'm not sure how I got here. Blind luck, I guess. Or fate."

The animals began to crowd around him, smelling him, staring at him.

"I'm sorry," the bear said. "But I think you can understand how having a human on the premises might be difficult."

"I've heard of this place. I've heard it's a respite from war. I didn't really believe it existed. In fact, I walked in the front door by accident. We've been told that animals don't like our vacated places. I had no idea I would find you here."

The bear reached down and patted the human's head. The human froze.

"Squirrel, set this man up with a bed. He needs rest."

From a nearby shelf, the squirrel, who had instinctively hidden from the human, squeaked his acquiescence and went about his work.

The bear looked the newcomer over carefully. "You remind me of another human," the bear said, "I met him a long time ago. I learned a great deal from him, although he never knew that."

The human almost smiled. "You're not the first animal I've talked to since I've been on my journey. But you have more to teach."

The bear nodded. The human reminded him of something else, something he couldn't quite identify.

Before the two could continue, another visitor surprised the room: a four-legged animal who burst in snarling, his charcoal mane frayed and matted with sweat and blood. His wild, iridescent eyes gleamed even in the pending dusk. The animal circled around the shivering human, and he howled.

The animals stood at attention.

"Wolf," someone said in an awed whisper.

"The human belongs to me," the animal said. "He is the enemy."

Several animals cheered.

"He belongs to no one," the bear replied. "We consider him a guest, as we do you. Can we get you something? Food? Drink?"

The animal looked out over the room. "I've heard of this place. The place the revolution forgot."

"We've been called many things. Some worse, some better."

"I have nothing against you, bear. But that human is mine." He took a step towards the human, who inched backwards, as did many of the other animals.

"Please eat," the bear said. One of the animals placed a dish of food before the newcomer. He sniffed it, but took none.

"I'm not here to eat. I'm here to kill."

"We don't kill in here."

"But he's *human*," the animal growled.

"He's no more at fault for being human than the mouse is for being a mouse or a bear a bear."

"I'm not going to argue. While you all sit here quietly, we are out there, fighting. Dying. For the sake of the revolution, and honor and loyalty, let me take the human."

Behind the bear a neat wall of animals had formed, listening and nodding. Now one of them stepped forward, like a brick falling out of place. A thin, scarred pig.

"Wolf," the pig said, "you have the look of a great warrior. Here you will find many animals who have had just as much of a quarrel with the humans as you do. None worse than me. I joined the revolution, I fought bitterly, and I realized that I had arrived at another hell. And I was so tired. So tired. Like you."

The newcomer looked confused and slightly irritated.

"What's your name, wolf?" the pig asked. "Mine is 323."

The cat, who until now had remained hidden in the shadows, stepped forward. "He's not a wolf. He's a dog."

The animal took a step back. He could feel scores of eyes staring not at him, but through him, trying to see where wolf ended and dog began. They all knew the stories of dogs who had taken the sides of the humans, who fought against them. Here was one who fought for them.

"His name is Cooper," the cat added. She stared at him, waiting for him to recognize her.

He started to speak, but it was as if the memory of his name, of the love he'd once felt when called by it, stopped him. He shook his dampened fur. He paced a bit, back and forth.

Then he said his name aloud—"Cooper"— and it hurt.

"Clio," he said to the cat. They stared at each other, each seeing in the others' eyes the worlds they had once known together, as well as how far they had grown apart. They both thought of a young woman.

"I won't do this again," Cooper said. "I can't."

"Do what?" Clio asked. She circled the dog, rubbing up against him the way she did when they were just two pets belonging to a friend. She purred.

"Let the humans get to me. Stop me from my task." He paused. "You were the one who made me go."

"I've grown up since then," Clio said.

"How many have you killed?" another animal asked.

The dog searched the crowd for the voice. It seemed to echo off the ceiling. He thought a bat might have spoken and he lowered his eyes defensively.

"I don't know. Many."

"Did killing any of them make you feel better?"

The dog, confused, didn't answer.

"I killed too, dog. I joined battles and fought and killed again. I tried to kill the right ones, but who can tell who deserves to die and who doesn't? You can't fix things by breaking them further."

The animal pushed her way into the light and stood next to the pig. The impossibly large grey elephant stood formidable and proud, her ears twitching slightly. .

A boom echoed from somewhere far away in the war, snapping the atmosphere. The animals shifted their stances.

The dog closed his eyes. He felt the warmth of the cat near his body, just as he had when he was a puppy, and now once more he thought of that woman, someone he suddenly wanted to see.

"Why don't you stay here for the night?" the bear asked. "Get some sleep."

"What about the humans? There's a party approaching. They were following me," the dog said.

"How many are there?" the bear asked.

"Plenty."

The animals burst into nervous chatter.

"Enough," the bear said, and the babble ceased.

The human spoke in a soft tremble. "Let me go. The humans. I can intercept them. I won't tell them about this place. Just say it's nothing but a wasteland. I can take them in another direction. And then I want to come back here."

"And why should we let you come back?" the bear asked.

The human exhaled. His body was emaciated; his skin seemed more yellow than flesh-toned. He opened his mouth to speak, but then closed it. "Because I'm tired, too," he finally said. He licked his lips, which were chapped and swollen. "I'm tired of the battle. And I know that you all must be, too."

"So you want to come back here so you can rest?" the bear asked.

"Not to rest," the human said. "To live. At first I didn't understand why you revolted against us. Now I do. I want to come back. This is where I should live. This is where we should all live."

The bear nodded.

"You would trust this human?" Cooper asked. "He will tell them where we are." He glanced around. "They will kill you. Every one of you."

"No. I will not do that," the human said.

The bear looked the human over. Every part of his new awareness and his old perception were at work, every sense, every thought. The human looked straight back at him.

"What do you think?" the bear asked the other animals.

A confused murmur arose. At last, the bear answered for the colony. "Yes," he said to the human. "But rest here tonight. You can leave tomorrow morning."

"No," the human replied. "They have the trail of the dog. They'll follow it. I have to go now and cut them off, lead them elsewhere. I don't know how I'll get back here, but I will."

The bear nodded. "Then let us feed you before you go."

The animals murmured their agreement, now that the bear had found it for them, and they offered food and water. As the others attended to the human, 323 trotted over to Cooper and Clio. The three of them talked about their pasts and their lives since awareness. The pig's soft, even tones calmed the dog, soothing his battle-scarred nerves. Clio occasionally licked the thicket of dirt and blood on her friend's back, and Cooper responded by doing something he hadn't done in a long time: He wagged his tail.

The bear and the elephant, whom the bear knew as Nancy, watched. "That pig is an unusually intelligent animal," the elephant said.

The bear nodded.

"Do you think the human will do as he says?" she asked.

"Everything depends on it," the bear replied.

"If he comes back, word will spread fast. It could make us a target. A human living among us."

"I would like to think of it as someone good living among others who are good," the bear said.

Nancy nodded. She leaned into the bear, just a little, so he could feel her weight upon him. In turn he leaned back against her for a few moments. Then, taking in a deep breath, he walked to the front of the store and rested one of his paws on the glass doors that he'd opened so many months ago. Outside, the wind swept loose leaves down the otherwise empty street. Some of them swirled up into an eddy, fell back to the asphalt, and then were picked up again and carried away.

Shifting his gaze, the bear saw in the reflection in the glass that the animals had moved. The pig was now resting comfortably on her haunches, talking to the elephant. The two animals laughed, which momentarily woke up the dog, who was lying next to them. He lifted his head, glanced around, realized there was no danger, and dropped his head back to the floor. The cat lay curled up next to him, eyes open. Next to her, the human was sitting on the floor, being fed by the squirrel.

The bear thought of the word "love," he thought of the word "creation," and he thought of his mother. He guessed that she would have liked it here, among the other animals in the colony. He imagined her, older and weaker, but still strong and noble, resting in the dusky aisles of the old human market, fattening up for winter, making jokes about the world, fate, her newfangled mind.

The noises outside, the sporadic sounds of war, were growing louder. But these commotions didn't concern the bear; he neither feared them nor ignored them. He had faith in his future—in their future. He watched the human reach toward the resting dog and stroke the animal in a manner that seemed to soothe both species, and he understood that the past and the future were bound to meet at the present. He walked over to the dog, the elephant, the pig, and the human, and stretched his arms to touch all of them as best he could. If the present was destined to find them, there was no place he'd rather be found.

Acknowledgements

The authors wish to thank
Edan Lepucki, Catie Disabato, Paul Bellaff, Linda Doyle,
Miranda Spencer, and Madeline McDonnell
for all their gracious help and guidance.

A special thanks to Luke Shanahan,
a great writer and a great friend.

About the Authors

Gene Stone (www.genestone.com) is a former
Peace Corps volunteer, journalist, and editor.
He is also the author or ghostwriter of thirty-five books,
including *Forks Over Knives*.

A graduate of Loyola Marymount University,
Jon Doyle has been a restaurateur, screenwriter,
and a journalist. This is his first novel.
He lives in Los Angeles.

CPSIA information can be obtained
at www.ICGtesting.com
Printed in the USA
LVHW031009300621
691472LV00010B/1324